Jill turned to face Megan. "I've been really rotten to everyone, Megan, especially you. I'm sorry." Jill's voice dropped almost to a whisper. "Can we still be best friends?" She was trying to smile, but her bottom lip quivered.

Megan hugged her tightly, and Jill hugged back. "It's okay, Jill," she said.

Jill leaned back. There was a tear running down her cheek. "It's just that sometimes I feel really down. I just keep thinking about what's wrong in my life..."

Jill and Megan began walking toward their lockers. "Sometimes it seems like my heart is too heavy for my body and it's pulling me down," Jill said. "I just don't feel like doing anything. And it's easier to stay angry at everybody, because then I can keep other feelings away. If I stop being angry, those feelings come back, and things get even worse."

Best Friends Don't Tell Lies

by Linda Barr

To my sister Gail—
who wishes more people
understood   depression

Published by Willowisp Press, Inc.
401 E. Wilson Bridge Road, Worthington, Ohio 43085

Printed in the United States of America

10 9 8 7 6 5 4 3 2

ISBN 0-87406-423-6

One

MEGAN watched as Jill carefully measured out the flour for the cookies they were making. The sun coming through the window made Jill's long blond hair glisten. Megan brushed a brown curl out of her own eyes and thought for the hundredth time how lucky she was to have Jill Walkerson for her best friend.

It's not just that she's beautiful and popular, Megan told herself. *It's that Jill really cares about me. If it weren't for her, I'd probably still be eating lunch by myself at school, like I did when Mom and I moved here from California last May. If it weren't for Jill, I'd still be watching reruns on TV every day after school, instead of practicing with the swim team for the big district meet.*

Jill started to mix the flour into the cookie dough. Megan opened a cupboard and pulled a cookie sheet from the jumble of baking pans.

They made so much noise banging together that she couldn't hear what Jill said.

"What did you say about your parents?" Megan asked.

"They're getting a divorce," Jill repeated quietly.

Megan's breath caught in her throat. She didn't know Jill's parents very well, but she knew how it felt to have your family fall apart in front of your eyes.

Megan swallowed hard. "Are you sure, Jill?"

Jill nodded as she picked up one of the cookie sheets. "I figured this was coming. They argued all the time, anyway. I don't know why Mom's acting so surprised about it."

Then Megan took a deep breath. "You're not going to move away, are you?"

Jill shook her head. "No, we'll be staying here—at least for now. My dad's moving to Dayton, though."

Boy, that was close, Megan thought as her heart pounded in relief. *Best friends aren't easy to find in the eighth grade. I don't think I could stand starting all over again.*

Jill poked at the cookie dough with a big spoon. "Do you think all of these ingredients are mixed enough?"

Megan glanced at the bowl, but she didn't answer. She wasn't thinking about the cookie dough. "I'm really glad you're not moving, Jill," she said. "But I know you must feel terrible. I remember how I felt when my dad moved out. I cried for three weeks straight. It got even worse when my mom's company asked her to move here and open a new office for them. I had to change schools and friends and everything. At least you don't have to change friends," Megan added with a little smile.

Jill nodded and started making balls out of the dough. Her long hair slipped forward and hid her face. Megan wished she could see if there were tears in Jill's eyes.

"When's your dad leaving?" Megan asked to break the silence.

"He's already gone," Jill stated bluntly. "He left last night."

Megan closed her eyes for a second. She knew she'd never forget the day after her own father left last spring. She remembered that she hadn't even gotten out of bed until it had started getting dark outside. Her mom had even come into her room to make her get up. Then they'd heated soup and hugged each other a lot. By the next morning, some of the scared feeling had left her stomach and she felt a tiny bit better.

"Did your dad take all his clothes with him?" Megan asked. Maybe Jill's father is just angry right now, and he'll be back later. He'll probably think things over and decide he'd rather be home with Jill and her mom.

"Yeah, he took everything. He even took his golf clubs," Jill said quietly.

Megan took a big breath. "Well, you know that Dayton is not too far away," she said. "You'll be able to see him all the time." Megan had spent two weeks last summer with her dad in California. She missed him—and Laurie and all her other friends at her old school. But she was starting to get used to being so far away from her old life. And being friends with Jill had helped her to adjust.

"Sure, I'll see my dad," Jill said as she put a fork on one of the dough balls and squashed it. "He's coming to get me this weekend. I'm going to stay with him in his new apartment." She squashed another ball flatter than the first one. "He'll miss the picture on Friday, but my mom's taking the afternoon off so she can come and be in it. You know her—she wouldn't miss that for the world."

I forgot all about the picture, Megan thought. Jill had been elected Student of the Month at Spring Middle School. The local newspaper was coming to school to take a picture of Jill and her parents.

Maybe that's why Jill doesn't seem that upset about her father's leaving. Besides her parents' problems, everything else in Jill's life was perfect. She's always on the honor roll.

8

And she's the best swimmer on our team. She even looks like a model.

Megan pulled in her stomach. *Maybe if my life were more like Jill's, it wouldn't have bothered me so much when my dad moved out,* she thought.

"At least you can still be on the swim team," Megan said in her most cheerful voice. "You and Nikki and Leah and I are going to win the relay for sure at the district meet next month."

"Yeah, sure," Jill mumbled. "My mom will like that, too. Maybe she'll get her picture in the newspaper again."

Jill seems pretty angry at her mother. She must be blaming her mother for the divorce. *I wish Jill would open up a little and talk with me about what she's feeling,* Megan thought.

Jill was making more dough balls, but they were getting smaller and smaller. Suddenly, Megan remembered that Jill's dad usually drove their team to all the swim meets.

"I saw you talking to Ryan after fourth period today," Megan said. She leaned closer to her friend. "He's so cute! What did he say?"

"Oh, something about going to a party."

"A party? That's great, Jill," Megan said. "When is it?"

Jill shrugged her shoulders. "I think it's in a couple of weeks." Then she looked up at Megan and smiled a little. "Oh, guess who was

9

asking about you in algebra today? It was Keith."

"Keith? Oh, how exciting." Megan said sarcastically. "Is that supposed to be good news?" She grabbed one of Jill's smaller dough balls and tossed it into her mouth.

"Come on, Megan. Keith's a nice guy," Jill said as she flattened another row of dough balls. "He's on the basketball team, and he's really smart, too. What more could you want?"

"How about someone who isn't seven feet tall and the worst klutz in the eighth grade?" Megan asked.

"Well, nobody's perfect," Jill said. She squashed the last dough ball, carried the cookie sheet over to the oven, and slid it inside. Then she stood there for a few seconds, rubbing her forehead with the back of her hand.

"Are you okay, Jill?" Megan asked softly.

"It's just a headache," Jill said. "I think I'll go on home."

"At least stay until the first batch of cookies is done," Megan suggested. "Then you can take some home for your parents—I mean, for you and your mother. Oh, I'm sorry, Jill."

"It's okay," Jill said with a sigh. "I'm not the first girl whose parents got divorced. It happens all the time, right?"

"Yeah, it does," Megan said assuredly. But

it doesn't happen all the time to you or me. She wanted to say that to Jill, to make her feel comforted somehow, but the words got caught in her throat.

They had just finished preparing another sheet of cookies for the oven when a sweet, burning smell filled the kitchen. Jill rushed over and yanked open the oven door.

"They're ruined!" she yelled.

Megan stood behind her friend and wrinkled her nose. "They're not that bad. They are just a little crispy around the edges."

Jill suddenly turned and glared at Megan. "Why didn't you set the timer?"

Megan took a step backward. "But you— oh, it doesn't matter, Jill. They look fine."

"No, they don't. I told you, they're ruined."

"No, they're not. Look at these in the middle of the sheet," Megan said, pointing to some of the cookies. But Jill had already grabbed her coat off the chair.

"I have to go," Jill said as she headed for the front door.

Megan pulled the cookie sheet out of the oven as the door slammed behind Jill. *I think the Walkersons' divorce is going to be hard on everyone,* she thought. *But Jill and I are best friends, both in fun times and in sad ones. I want her to be happy again, like she's made me. So, I'll do whatever I can to help her get through this mess.*

The next day at lunch, Megan, Nikki, and Leah waited for Jill to show up at their usual table in the noisy school cafeteria.

"Do you want my cupcake, Megan?" Leah asked as she tossed it to her. Then Leah chose a little white squiggle from a pile of white squiggles in front of her and popped it into her mouth. "You know, if I eat these bean sprouts one at a time, I'll feel really full and probably lose at least two pounds today."

Nikki and Megan looked at each other and smiled. Leah, who always looked thin to Megan, had lost and gained the same five pounds at least three times since Megan had met her last May. Sometimes it seemed like Leah's diets began at breakfast and ended when she sat down for dinner.

"Where is Jill today, anyway?" Nikki asked. "We need to plan an extra practice time."

Jill was the best swimmer on their team, but Nikki was the captain. She and Jill and Leah had swum together on the relay team last year, too, but the fourth girl had moved to Michigan last spring. That's when Jill had invited Megan to swim with them. Their team had finished in second place at the district meet last year. This time they planned to win, not only at the district meet, but also at the state meet a month afterward.

"Maybe Jill's getting her picture taken with her parents now," Leah suggested.

"The picture's tomorrow," Megan told them. "And only Jill's mom is coming." Then Megan filled them in on what was happening with Jill's parents.

"That poor kid! That's rotten news," Nikki said. "She never said anything about her parents having problems or anything. How was she this morning, Megan, when you two walked to school?"

"This is Thursday," Megan said. "Jill always walks to school early on Thursday for her flute lesson. And I haven't seen her in school anywhere yet."

"Ah! I've found an empty seat. What tremendous luck I have," a male voice said. Suddenly, he slid into the seat beside Megan. She looked over and saw that it was Keith. She glanced around the cafeteria and saw empty seats at half the tables. She also caught Nikki and Leah hiding their grins behind their hands. Why does everyone think Keith is cute?

Megan sighed and turned her face toward Keith. "Did you see Jill in algebra class?" she asked him.

"Nope." Keith stuffed half his sandwich in his mouth, chewed twice, and swallowed hard.

"Jill wasn't there today. It's too bad, too. We had a test. Hey, are those homemade?"

He grabbed a cookie and shoved it into his mouth.

"They're delicious," he mumbled as crumbs tumbled down his chin.

Megan shook her head in disbelief. She did not find Keith cute at all. *Well, at least I know that Jill wasn't in algebra. She must not have come to school today. She must be sick,* Megan thought.

During her walk home after swim practice, Megan decided to stop by Jill's house. She rang the doorbell and waited. Then she rang it again. Finally, as she turned to leave, the door opened a crack.

"Megan," Jill almost whispered. "It's you."

Jill's hair stuck together in little clumps, the way it had last summer when they went camping and forgot their shampoo. She had big gray circles under her eyes.

"Are you sick, Jill?" Megan asked.

Jill shook her head. "No, it's just this terrible headache. I couldn't sleep last night. I'll call you later, Megan, okay?" She pushed the door shut.

Megan stood facing the closed door. *Jill didn't even ask me to come inside,* she thought. *She really must be feeling badly to do that. I wonder if it's the same headache she had yesterday. I just wish she'd tell me what's going on, so I could help her.*

Megan walked home slowly, taking her time to shuffle through the leaves that were piling up everywhere. Suddenly, as the leaves were floating in the air, Megan remembered that Jill had hit her head the week before when she'd slipped on the wet tile by the pool. The spot had swelled up at first, but Jill had insisted that she was all right.

That bump could be giving her headaches now.

By 9:30 that night, Megan couldn't stand to wait any longer for Jill to call. She dialed the Walkersons' number. Jill's mom answered on the third ring and said that Jill was already in bed.

"Is she feeling any better?" Megan asked, trying to keep her voice calm.

"Jill's doing just fine," her mom said. "In fact, we're both...I mean, we're all just fine. She decided to go to bed a little early tonight, that's all. She'll see you in school tomorrow."

After Megan hung up the phone, she wondered if Jill's mom knew that Jill hadn't gone to school. She wondered if Jill had even told her mom that she'd had a headache for two days. *I'll bet she didn't*, Megan thought, *because she doesn't seem to share much of anything with her mom. Come to think of it, Jill doesn't share much with anyone these days—not even with me.*

Two

O N Friday morning, Megan was relieved when she saw Jill waiting for her at their usual corner to walk to school together. She decided not to mention Jill's fall near the pool.

I'm sure my imagination is just working overtime, Megan told herself. *Everyone has headaches and feels badly sometimes—even best friends.*

At lunchtime, though, Jill sat silently and stared at her sandwich.

"What do you think?" Nikki asked her teammates with a smile. "Will they give us one big trophy or four small ones when we win the relay race?"

"How about four big ones?" Megan suggested.

"I just wish we could wear our own bathing suits," Leah said, looking around the table at the girls. "Hey, I know! Why don't you all buy suits like mine? Then we could match."

Nikki and Megan rolled their eyes, but Jill didn't seem to be listening to their conversation.

"Why doesn't the school hire teachers with some brains?" Jill muttered.

"What's wrong, Jill?" Nikki asked.

"I got my language paper back today," Jill told her.

"So?" Leah asked with a grin. "Did you get an A- instead of an A+ this time?"

"No, that isn't it. Mrs. Bell wants me to do it over," Jill told them.

Megan couldn't believe her ears. "You?" she asked. "A teacher wants *you* to do a paper over? I can't believe it."

"She says that the paper wasn't up to my usual high standards."

"Mrs. Bell must be having a bad day," Megan told her. She knew that teachers used Jill's papers as examples in classes all the time.

Jill grabbed her sandwich and took a bite out of it. "Oh, who cares, anyway? Grades aren't the most important thing in the world."

Nikki, Leah, and Megan looked across the table at each other and ate the rest of their lunches in silence

By the time Megan and Jill walked home after school, Jill had calmed down. "Do you think I should wear my hair down or in a

French braid?" she asked.

"Didn't they already take your picture for the newspaper?" Megan asked.

Jill nodded impatiently. "Yes, they did. I'm talking about how I should wear my hair for when my dad comes to pick me up tonight."

"Jill, your dad already knows what you look like."

Jill ignored her. "Maybe I'll go with the French braid. He always likes my hair that way."

Megan took Jill's hand. "Jill," she said softly. "Your parents' divorce isn't your fault. Your dad loves you for who you are. You don't have anything to prove to him."

"I know," Jill said quietly. "But I still want to look nice for him. Maybe he'll take me shopping in Dayton."

"Yeah, I guess they have some nice stores there," Megan agreed. The thought of Jill and her dad doing things together made Megan suddenly miss her own father. It seemed like years since she had seen him.

Later that night, Megan was watching some music videos on TV when the phone rang in the kitchen. "I'll get it," she told her mom. *I bet it's Dad,* she thought.

Her mom looked up from the cross-stitch pillow she was working on. "It's 10:15," she said. "I hope this isn't some kind of obscene call. Maybe I should answer it, Megan."

"I can handle it," Megan assured her.

"Hello?" Megan said into the phone.

No one said anything. There didn't seem to be anybody there. *Dad would have said something back*, Megan thought. *He wouldn't play these stupid kinds of jokes on me.*

"Hello," she repeated in her most adult voice.

"He's not coming," a voice whispered finally. It was Jill.

"Why? What happened, Jill?"

"My dad's still staying in a hotel. There's no room for me to stay with him."

Megan could hear the pain in her best friend's voice. She wondered if Jill's father knew how much she had been looking forward to seeing him. She wondered if her own father knew how much she still missed him.

"I'm sorry, Jill. Do you...do you want to sleep over here tonight?" she asked. "We could make fudge and..."

"No, I'm all right." Jill's voice got louder. "It's no big thing, anyway. I'll probably go there next weekend."

"At least now you can come to the movies with Nikki and Leah and me tomorrow," Megan suggested.

"No, I'm busy. My mom...oh, nothing. Maybe we can do something another time."

Then Jill hung up.

Megan listened to the dial tone for a moment, and then she put the phone down, too. *Maybe I should go over there and make sure Jill really is okay,* she thought. *Jill is trying to pretend that the divorce and her father's canceling out are not important. But I know her a lot better than that. I know that she's really hurting inside. I wish I could do something for her.*

Megan thought of a time last spring right after she and Jill had met. Jill's puppy had been hit by a car and killed. They had been trying to catch him when he ran into the street. Megan could still picture Jill sitting on the curb, holding the puppy's limp body on her lap, and petting him. Jill didn't cry then, either.

But I did, Megan remembered.

"Who was it?" Mrs. Schuster called from the living room.

"It was Jill," Megan said.

"At this time of night? What did she want?" her mother asked.

"I'm not sure." Megan dropped down on the couch beside her mother. "Her parents are getting a divorce. And I'm not really sure how Jill's taking the whole thing."

Her mother's needle stopped in mid-stitch. For a minute Mrs. Schuster stared into space without saying anything. "I guess Jill must be upset naturally," she finally said.

"I guess she is," Megan said. "But it's hard to tell. She doesn't seem like her old self a lot of the time, but she's not crying about it, either. It's really weird."

"Jill will need a friend now, Megan. It's a good thing she has you," her mom said.

Megan thought for a moment. "I don't know, though. I want to do something to help, but Jill doesn't seem to want to talk about it or share her feelings with me."

Mrs. Schuster reached over and patted her daughter's hand. "Jill will get through this, you'll see. You know what it was like for us. It took a while, but we've come a long way. She'll feel better next week and even better the week after. It's just hard to get used to at first. Remember?"

Megan nodded. *I remember. And I hope Mom's right*, she thought. *Maybe as the date for the swim meet gets closer, Jill will be able to concentrate on that. Maybe she'll be able to forget about her dad, at least for a little while. She wants to win the meet this year, just as much as Nikki, Leah, and I do. Well, at least she used to.*

Three

ON Monday, Jill wasn't waiting at the corner to walk to school with Megan. And she didn't show up for her morning classes. As Megan sat down with Nikki and Leah at lunchtime, she began to worry again.

"Maybe Jill has a headache again," Leah suggested.

I almost forgot about the headaches, Megan realized. *Could it be Jill's fall by the pool that is causing all of this?*

"Do you remember a couple of weeks ago," Megan began, "when Jill slipped near the pool and hit her head?"

They both nodded.

"Well, do you think that fall could have anything to do with Jill's headaches now? I mean, maybe she really hurt her head and has a blood clot or something."

Nikki thought for a minute. "I don't think so. She seemed fine after the fall. And the

22

coach wasn't worried about it."

"But maybe it takes a while for a blood clot to do any damage," Megan suggested. "And remember in health class, when the teacher told us that brain tumors can change someone's personality? Maybe a blood clot could be making Jill kind of hard to get along with."

"Kind of hard to get along with?" Leah repeated sarcastically. She poked her fork at her lunch of plain lettuce and diet dressing.

"She's just being that way because she's upset about her parents' divorce, Megan," Nikki assured her. "That's all. She'll get over it pretty soon." Nikki nibbled on a cookie. "You know, if she's not in school today, she probably won't be at swim practice after school, either. That will make two practices in a row she's missed. That's a lot, even for a good swimmer like Jill."

Leah nodded. "I hope she can make it," she mumbled with a mouthful of lettuce. "We sure need her if we're going to win."

"I'll call and see how she is," Megan offered. "Maybe she'll feel good enough to come to practice today."

She hurried to the pay phone, but when she dialed Jill's number, she got a busy signal. Who could she be calling? Her friends are all at school. Maybe her mom stayed home from work with her. Yeah, that's it. Her mom must be calling the doctor to make sure Jill is okay.

Megan breathed a sigh of relief. After her next class, though, the line was still busy. She tried to call two more times that afternoon. The line was busy both times.

Finally, it was the last class of the day—Spanish, where the teacher hardly ever spoke a word of English. *Mrs. Sanchez must be telling us to open our books,* Megan thought as she looked around the room.

Out of the corner of her eye, Megan could see Keith grinning at her. He sat next to her every afternoon in Spanish. It was the only class they had together. Thank goodness.

She looked over at him and realized he was grinning because she was on the wrong page. She leaned toward him a little to see which page he was pointing to.

"You owe me one," Keith whispered.

Megan just sighed and ignored him.

At swim practice after school, Coach White marked Jill down as absent again. He assigned another girl to Megan, Nikki, and Leah's team for a practice relay race. They always came in first in these practice runs, but that day they had to struggle to place second.

Afterward in the locker room, Nikki and Leah got dressed in silence.

"I'll stop at Jill's house on my way home,"

Megan offered. "I'll tell her she has to start coming to practice, even if she does have a headache. Maybe she'll be happy that she was missed so much."

"She'd better be here tomorrow," Nikki said glumly. "Or we can just forget about winning the swim meet. Remind her that we have practice tomorrow."

As Megan turned the corner and Jill's house came into view, she was surprised that Mrs. Walkerson's car wasn't in the driveway. She rang the doorbell and waited. Just as she pressed it a second time, the door flew open and banged against the wall behind it.

Jill stood in the doorway grinning and wearing one of her father's old T-shirts over a pair of jeans. Then she staggered backward a step. She grabbed the door frame to keep her balance. "Hi," Jill said in a slurred voice.

Megan stared at her friend. She opened her mouth to say something, but no words came out.

Jill just kept smiling. "Yep, I've been drinking Mom's rum. I talked to Ryan at school, and he was right. I haven't felt this good in weeks." She tried to point to her head, but ended up pointing to her ear. "There's no headache left." Then she leaned closer to Megan.

The smell of Jill's breath made Megan take

a step backward. Megan couldn't believe that Ryan would tell her that drinking would make her feel better.

Then Jill broke into Megan's thoughts. "There's no pain at all. I don't feel a thing," Jill whispered hoarsely.

She turned and lurched toward the living room. Megan quickly stepped inside and pulled the door shut before the neighbors had the chance to see what was happening.

"Jill, what are...," Megan began, but she heard a disgusting coughing sound and knew it was already too late.

Megan rushed into the living room. Jill had thrown up on the carpet. She stood unsteadily over the mess with a surprised look on her face. "I think I'll go to bed now," Jill mumbled.

Megan practically carried Jill upstairs and put her to bed, jeans and all. Then, trying not to gag, she cleaned up the rug as well as she could. The smell made her own stomach turn as she rinsed out the towels she had used to clean up the mess. *I need to find some air freshener,* she thought. *And then everything will be okay.*

She searched through the kitchen cupboards and only found lemon-scented furniture polish. She decided it would work if she couldn't find anything else. Just as she turned to check out the downstairs bathroom, she noticed that the phone was off the hook.

She put the phone back in place, hurried upstairs to Jill's room, and grabbed a bottle of her perfume. Jill was snoring, her blond hair tangled on the pillow. Megan sprayed the perfume around the bedroom and then went back downstairs. She was spraying perfume around the living room when she heard a car pull into the driveway. *Oh, no,* Megan thought, *it's Mrs. Walkerson!*

Megan slid the perfume under the couch and hurried into the kitchen just as Mrs. Walkerson came in the back door.

"Megan! What a surprise!"

Megan smiled uncertainly.

"Jill, I'm home!" her mother called. "Megan, is that a new kind of perfume you're wearing?"

"Uh, yes," Megan stammered. "Do you like it?"

Mrs. Walkerson nodded and smiled. "Jill!" she called again.

"Uh, Jill's sick, Mrs. Walkerson. She's sleeping right now. I was just going home," Megan replied quickly.

Jill's mom frowned. "What's wrong? Is she having headaches again?"

"Yeah, that's it," Megan agreed.

So, Jill's mom does know about the headaches. Knowing Jill, the headaches must be bad for her to tell her mom about them.

"Jill just needs some sleep. I wouldn't even bother checking on her. I mean, she doesn't have a fever or anything."

Mrs. Walkerson looked at Megan. "Well, I still think I should see how she's doing."

She started up the stairs. Megan waited at the bottom of the steps, holding her breath. She heard Mrs. Walkerson open Jill's door and then close it a few seconds later.

"She's sound asleep," Jill's mother said as she came back downstairs. "You girls have sure been into the perfume this afternoon, haven't you?"

Megan smiled nervously. "Yeah, I guess maybe we overdid it."

Mrs. Walkerson took off her coat and hung it in the hall closet. "Jill probably told you that I made a doctor's appointment for her this Friday. I want to ask Dr. Simmons about the headaches she's been having."

"A doctor's appointment?" Megan repeated. "That's great because a couple of weeks ago—"

"Yeah, I know that they have been going on for a while," Mrs. Walkerson interrupted. "Maybe Jill has a sinus problem or something. She's usually very healthy, you know, and being on the swim team is great exercise."

It's good exercise if you show up for practices, Megan thought.

"Jill is so careful about what she eats, too, just like her father," Mrs. Walkerson said.

Megan realized that Jill's mom was pretending for her benefit. *She doesn't know that Jill told me about the divorce and about her father moving to Dayton*, Megan thought. *She's still pretending that everything is okay.*

During the short walk home, Megan felt sick herself. She thought she could smell vomit on her clothes.

How much had Jill drunk? And why did she do it? She had mentioned Ryan. Had it been his idea? *Maybe I should have tried harder to tell Mrs. Walkerson about Jill hitting her head at the pool*, Megan worried. *I bet Jill didn't tell her.*

But Mrs. Walkerson is right about one thing. Jill usually does take really good care of herself. She eats right. In fact, she's always bugging Leah about the terrible diets she goes on. So, why then would she gorge herself with a bottle of booze? It's just not like Jill at all. *It's not like my best friend to care so little about herself.* What would Jill's mom think if she knew Jill had been drinking all afternoon?

Megan wondered what was going to happen. When Jill woke up, she'd surely have the worst headache of her life. Would she skip out on school again? What about swim practice? If Jill missed a third time, the coach would probably take some action against her. Maybe he'd even replace her on their team. Then there would be no way they'd win at the state meet.

Boy, I wish her appointment with Dr. Simmons was tomorrow, Megan thought. *I want her to be my best friend again.*

Four

THE next morning Jill was waiting at the corner. They walked to school together— in silence. Megan figured she'd better not ask how Jill was feeling.

After a while, Jill slowed down and didn't make any effort to keep up. Megan finally stopped for the third time and looked back over her shoulder. Jill was almost half a block behind her. Then Megan noticed that Jill wasn't carrying any books.

"Jill, if you walk any slower, first period will be over before we get to the next corner!" Megan called.

"Who cares?" Jill yelled back. "So what if we're late. I can be late once in my life."

"Well, I already was late more than once in my life," Megan told her. "And I'm going to get in trouble if it happens again."

"So, go on without me then. I really don't care," Jill snapped.

"Jill!" Megan walked back to meet Jill. "I want to walk with you. And I want to talk to you, too."

"What do you want to talk to me about?" Jill asked as she started walking a little faster.

Megan sighed. This wasn't going to be easy. *Maybe if I start slowly and build up to talking about the rum.* "How do you feel today?" Megan asked her.

"I feel terrific," Jill said through clenched teeth. Her eyes were really bloodshot.

"Well, if you've forgotten what happened yesterday, I haven't," Megan blurted out. Suddenly, she felt like crying. This wasn't the way best friends talked to each other. What was happening to them?

Megan grabbed Jill's arm to make her stop walking. "Promise me you won't get drunk like that again, Jill, please?" she begged.

Jill put her hands on her hips and stared at the sidewalk. "I won't promise anything."

"Why not?" Megan asked. "Was that so much fun? You threw up all over the rug. I can see that you feel terrible today. Why would you want to do that to yourself again?"

"You just don't understand, Megan."

"Understand? I understand that we used to be best friends. That's what I understand."

For the first time that morning, Jill looked straight at Megan. The angry lines between her eyes softened and disappeared. "I guess I can't explain how I feel right now." She shook her head. "But I really do need you to be my best friend, Megan."

"If you mean that, then promise you won't get drunk again," Megan insisted.

"I—I can't. I can't promise anything."

"Jill, I might not be around to clean up the mess next time, you know."

Jill suddenly glared at her. "That's just a chance I'll have to take, isn't it?"

Megan felt tears burning in her eyes, and she couldn't say anything else. Jill must have seen the tears, because she put her arms around Megan and hugged her. Megan gratefully hugged her back.

"Oh, Megan, I'm sorry," Jill said with a big sigh as she pulled back. "But yesterday, for a while at least, I felt really good. I felt better than I have since..."

"But I've been there, too. I know what you're going through," Megan said.

Jill pulled back. "What am I going through? My parents are getting divorced, that's all! It's no big deal!"

Then Megan noticed that Jill put her hands up to her temples and rubbed them.

"You have another headache, don't you? At least tell your mother about the time you slipped and hit your head at the pool," Megan urged. She put her hand on Jill's arm. "Maybe that's why you have those headaches. Of course, today, maybe there's another reason."

Jill looked so angry that Megan pulled her hand back. "I'd be just fine if everyone would get off my back!" Jill yelled. She turned and hurried up the road toward school. By the time Megan got her notebooks from her locker, she was late to class again.

Jill might need a best friend, but she's not making it easy on me, Megan thought as she sat in her first class. At lunchtime, Megan waited for Jill by the lockers. *I hope she's calmed down some,* Megan thought, *because I need to remind her about swim team practice today. If she misses another one, Nikki and Leah are really going to be upset.*

"I'll bet you're looking for Jill again," Keith said from behind her.

Oh, boy, Megan thought. *I'm losing my best friend, and this geek won't leave me alone.*

"This time I know where Jill is," he said.

Megan looked up at him. "Where?" she asked, trying not to sound worried.

"She's taking a makeup test for algebra," he told her. "It's a tough one, too. Even *I* almost got a *B*."

"How awful for you," Megan replied.

He leaned closer to Megan. "You know, I heard about Jill's parents. It's too bad. How

34

is she taking it? She sure has missed algebra a lot lately."

Megan glared at him. "She'll be fine, Keith."

"Okay, okay." He held up his big hands. "Forget that I asked." He turned and pushed his way down the crowded hallway.

Megan felt bad for being so rude to Keith. She wanted to protect Jill from everyone. Her instinct was to shield her from any other problems that came along. *Yeah, but then I'll be as hard to get along with as Jill is,* Megan thought.

Megan didn't see Jill until swim practice after school. As Megan hurried from the locker room to the pool area, she spotted Jill leaning against a wall and staring at her bare feet while the coach talked to her.

Megan breathed a sigh of relief that Jill had even shown up. The huge room echoed with voices and splashing water, so Megan couldn't hear what the coach was saying—even though she wanted to. She guessed he was telling Jill that she'd better come to practice or be replaced on the team.

Jill didn't even look up when the coach patted her shoulder and walked away. Then the coach blew his whistle and announced they would be swimming a practice relay race.

"Okay, team," Nikki said as the four girls gathered by their usual starting block. "Let's

show them how we're going to win the meet."
Nikki looked straight at Jill, but Jill was still staring at her feet.

As they lined up for the relay, Megan leaned closer to Jill. "I'm glad you're here," she whispered.

Jill sighed. "Yeah," she said in a flat voice. "I guess I am, too."

The coach blew his whistle again, and the race started. Leah dived in to swim the first leg of the relay. The room filled with ear-splitting screeches as each team cheered on its first swimmer.

While Megan waited to swim the third leg of the relay, she shook her arms to loosen her muscles. Standing beside her, Jill was staring into space with her arms crossed. She looks like she's waiting for a bus. Was it really only two or three weeks ago that Jill gave us all a pep talk? She had encouraged us to use all of our strength to win this year.

We'll go on to the state meet, Jill had promised. We are the best team this school has ever seen!

And now Jill wasn't even watching the race.

Megan wasn't surprised at all that Jill struggled to finish her laps. Their team finished dead last. Megan glanced over at Nikki and Leah. Both were watching silently as pool water dripped off their hair and down their shoulders. Nikki was frowning, her eyebrows meeting in a dark line. Leah was chewing on her lip. Jill put one arm in the pool gutter to hold herself up while she tried to catch her breath. Megan finally knelt down and helped her climb out of the pool.

"Okay, team!" the coach yelled to everyone. "It's time to do laps. Let's get that endurance up!"

Jill sat on the edge of the pool, with her head down, her chest still heaving. Megan saw the coach stare at Jill for a long minute.

About 10 minutes later, Megan stopped at the end of a lap and floated on her back for a minute. She lifted her head to look for Jill's blond head in the water, but she didn't see her in the pool or anywhere nearby. Where could she have gone?

The coach blew his whistle again to signal that practice was over. One by one, the swimmers pulled their tired bodies out of the pool and headed for the showers. Someone tapped Megan on the shoulder. "What happened to Jill?" Nikki asked angrily. Her voice was quiet and low, but she was definitely upset.

"I don't know," Megan admitted. "But she's having a hard time."

"I know she is!" Nikki blurted out. "And I'm sorry about that. But my parents invited my whole family to watch us in the district meet. I should just tell them all to stay home." Nikki turned and stomped toward the showers. Leah followed her.

She's right. Maybe we all should stay home.

Then Megan headed for the showers, too. Where could Jill be? We'll never win if she keeps ducking out early or not showing up at all.

Jill wasn't waiting in the locker room, either. And Nikki and Leah lived in the opposite direction, so Megan ended up walking home by herself. She pulled up the zipper on her coat all the way to her chin to try to keep the cold out.

Here I am walking home all alone, just like when I moved here, Megan thought bitterly. *Wherever Jill is, I guess it hasn't occurred to her that I might need a best friend, too.*

Five

MEGAN took her time on the walk home. She stopped in the park and watched some kids playing.

As soon as she unlocked the front door to her home, she heard the phone ringing. She ran to answer it.

It was Jill's mother calling from her office. "You're finally home!" Mrs. Walkerson sounded relieved. "I've been calling for half an hour. Can I talk to Jill, please? I'm going to be late, and I need to give her a message."

"Jill's not here."

"She isn't? Where is she then? There was no answer when I called home. Didn't you have swim practice together this afternoon?"

"Well, yes, but Jill.... Maybe she's at home now," Megan suggested. *Oh, no, where could she be?* Megan took a big breath and tried to keep her voice steady. "I'll go over to your house and see if she's there, Mrs. Walkerson.

I'll tell her to call you, okay?"

"Megan, is something wrong?"

"Oh, no, it's nothing," Megan said quickly. "Good-bye."

Megan dropped her books and raced out of her house. The two blocks to Jill's house flew by. It was starting to get dark, but she could see Jill's house now. There didn't seem to be any lights on. But if Jill wasn't home, then where was she?

Megan stopped at the front door and peered inside the narrow window beside the door. She could see the stairs that led up to the bedrooms and the door to the kitchen. There was a faint glow coming from the kitchen. Maybe Jill was in there. Megan pushed the doorbell.

There was no answer. Megan pushed the doorbell again.

Something moved in the shadows at the top of the stairs. It was Jill, but what was she doing? Why didn't she turn on the lights?

Then Megan watched in horror as Jill started down the steps and fell, tumbling over and over until she lay in a quiet heap at the bottom of the stairs.

Megan tried to yank the front door open, but it was locked. Then Megan remembered that Jill's family always kept a key hidden beneath a rock in the flower garden near the front steps. Megan quickly started turning over rocks. She glanced in the window again. Jill hadn't moved.

Megan clawed at the rocks in the flower bed. Where was the key? Just then, headlights flashed in her eyes as a car turned into the driveway. It was Mrs. Walkerson.

Megan stumbled through the flower bed to the car. She pulled the car door open before Jill's mom could ask what was happening.

"Jill fell," Megan gasped, bracing herself against the car door with one muddy hand. "The front door's locked."

Mrs. Walkerson grabbed her keys from the ignition and ran to the front door. In seconds they were in the house. Just as they knelt beside Jill, she moaned a little. *Thank God*, Megan thought. *Jill isn't dead.*

"Don't move, Jill," her mother said. "You might be hurt." She gently ran her hand along the back of Jill's neck. "How did this happen? What were you doing here in the dark?"

Jill pushed her mother's hand away and tried to sit up. Megan saw a puddle of blood on the floor. Suddenly, the dim hallway seemed to Megan to be getting even blacker. Megan's head seemed to be floating away from her body. She quickly sat down and put her forehead against her knees to keep from fainting. Mrs. Walkerson must have seen the blood, too, because she crouched behind Jill and looked at the back of her head.

"There's a big gash here," Jill's mother said in a surprisingly steady voice. "We better call an ambulance."

"No," Jill moaned. "I'm okay." Her words were thick and slurred.

Then Megan noticed the smell. It smelled like rum again. She glanced over at Mrs. Walkerson, who stood frozen in place with a streak of blood on one outstretched hand. She stared at her daughter.

She smells the rum, too, Megan thought.

Jill tried to sit up again. Jill's movement seemed to unfreeze her mother. "Megan, go call an ambulance." Her voice sounded dead. "Dial 911. There's a phone in the kitchen."

"I'm okay," Jill insisted groggily. "My head just hurts." She moved one unsteady hand toward her head. "It always hurts."

"Go ahead, Megan," Mrs. Walkerson commanded.

Megan hurried into the kitchen and dialed 911. Her throat was so dry that she could barely talk to the operator. "My friend fell," she managed to say. Then she couldn't remember Jill's address.

"It's okay," the operator said calmly. "I can trace the call to tell where you are. Just calm down. The ambulance is already on its way."

It was only minutes before she heard a siren in the distance. Megan found the light switch for the front hallway and flipped it on. Jill waved her hand against the sudden brightness and muttered something to herself. Her mother sat holding onto Jill's other hand.

During the drive to the hospital, Megan rode in the front seat of the ambulance with the driver. Mrs. Walkerson and a paramedic were in back with Jill, who was strapped down to a stretcher. A strap across Jill's forehead kept her head from moving.

"She is going to be okay, isn't she?" Mrs. Walkerson was asking the paramedic. Her voice was shaky now. "My husband—you don't have to call him. I've got a card for the insurance. She's all right, isn't she?" Then Megan heard a muffled sound like crying.

Suddenly, Jill's mom cried out, "Is she breathing?"

Megan jerked around to see what was happening, but the paramedic said, "She's sleeping. Please calm down."

When they got to the hospital, the paramedics pulled Jill's stretcher out of the ambulance and unfolded its legs. Then they pushed it through a door marked "No Entry."

After that, nothing happened for a long time. Megan tried to watch the TV in the waiting room while Mrs. Walkerson filled out some forms. Everything seemed to be taking forever. Finally, Jill's mom came out and sat down beside Megan. Her eyes were bloodshot and teary.

"How is she?" Megan asked.

"She just needs some stitches, that's all. It was an accident. It was so dark on those stairs." Mrs. Walkerson kept straightening her skirt as she talked. Her hands were shaking. "They'll have to shave off some of her hair to do the stitches." Jill's mom shook her head sadly. "That beautiful hair. Her father..." She stopped talking and looked up at Megan.

"Megan, why don't you call your mom? Maybe she could come and pick you up. You don't need to worry about Jill. Everything's okay now." She patted Megan's arm and forced a smile. But Megan noticed that there was still the look of panic in her eyes.

Megan wanted to yell at her. She wanted to tell Jill's mom that everything was not okay. Jill doesn't get drunk and fall down the stairs every day. Megan just had to say something.

"Uh, Mrs. Walkerson..."

"Do you need some money for the phone?" Jill's mom fumbled in her purse and pulled out her wallet.

"I guess I do," Megan realized. She had left her own purse at her house when she ran out. It seemed like days ago.

44

Megan took the quarter Mrs. Walkerson handed her, but she didn't get up. *I've got to talk to her about the way Jill's been acting lately*, Megan decided, *and about her fall at the pool and her drinking. But how do I start?* she wondered.

"Uh, Mrs. Walkerson, do you think Jill has been kind of hard to get along with lately?"

Mrs. Walkerson looked away. "You know how it is. Everyone has bad days sometimes. Jill's excited about the swim meet."

No, she isn't, Megan wanted to scream.

"And her dad has...been away quite a bit lately." Mrs. Walkerson turned to Megan and smiled as brightly as she could. "I guess it all adds up. But if anyone can handle it, Jill can. She'll be fine, you'll see. She's a super girl."

"But Jill doesn't seem..."

Mrs. Walkerson quickly stood up and looked around the waiting room. "I see some phones over there, Megan." She pointed toward the corner. "Do you know the number?" Then she gave a nervous little laugh. "Oh, of course you do. What am I thinking of?"

Megan realized that talking with Mrs. Walkerson was pointless, so she walked over to the phone to call her mom.

Megan's mother answered the phone right away. She had begun to search for clues to her own daughter's whereabouts. The door to their home had been left unlocked, and Megan's school books were scattered on the floor near the phone.

During the ride home, Megan told her mother about Jill's fall and about her drinking.

Her mother shook her head. "Well, I hate to see it happen, but I guess some kids just have to experiment with drinking," her mother said.

"She wasn't experimenting, Mom!"

"Megan, I know that lots of kids try out different things just to see what happens. If I were Jill's mother, I would watch her to be sure that she doesn't keep on drinking. But I think Jill's too smart to do that, just like I think you are too smart to start drinking."

Smart is not exactly the word to describe Jill's behavior lately. But maybe Mom's right about the drinking being part of a phase that she's going through.

Megan rested her head against the back of the seat and was almost asleep when another thought woke her up again. Maybe the hospital will do an X-ray of Jill's head. That will show whether her fall at the pool is causing her headaches or not.

Then I won't have to worry anymore about whether to tell Mrs. Walkerson or not. The truth will be out. Megan sighed her relief.

Six

"YOU'RE late, Megan," Jill called to her. Jill was standing at the corner the next morning with her arms folded across her chest.

"Jill, give me a break! I didn't think you'd be here," Megan said as she hurried to the corner. "Don't you need to stay in bed today or anything?"

"Why would I need to do that?" Jill asked as she started walking toward school.

Was Jill trying to just ignore all that happened? Megan suddenly felt like shaking her. She grabbed Jill's arm. "Let me see the back of your head, Jill," she demanded.

Jill rolled her eyes, but she turned around. Behind one ear, in the middle of a shaved patch of skin, was a row of stitches that looked like black spiders standing in line. Some clear, shiny covering protected the stitches.

"Do you remember getting stitches last night?" Megan asked.

"Megan, I just tripped on the stairs. It was an accident," Jill said.

"That's all that happened, huh?" Megan asked. She felt herself getting more angry. "So, you're telling me that you weren't drinking again, right?"

Jill looked at Megan for at least a minute without answering. Her defiance finally faded away when she saw that Megan wasn't going to back down.

"Yes, I was drinking," Jill almost whispered. "Drinking makes my headaches go away. If you really were my best friend, you'd want me to feel better any way I can." She turned toward the school and started walking again.

Megan stared at Jill's back as they walked along.

"Wait, Jill!" Megan hurried to catch up. "Did they do an X-ray of your head last night?"

Jill shook her head. "It was just a small cut—no big deal. Come on." She started to walk faster. "We're going to be late."

As they hurried down the sidewalk, Megan glanced sideways at Jill. *I bet she can't remember whether she had an X-ray or not.*

At least Jill still had her appointment with Dr. Simmons coming up on Friday. *Maybe he'd get to the bottom of her headache problem*, Megan thought.

At lunchtime Nikki and Leah wanted to

hear all about how Jill got her stitches. *Please don't bring up the swim team issue*, Megan silently begged.

"But how did you fall?" Nikki kept asking.

"I just slipped in the dark," Jill said again. She unwrapped her sandwich.

Megan stuffed a cookie into her mouth. *How can you sit here and lie to them so easily, Jill?* she wanted to scream.

Nikki turned to Megan. "You were there, right, Megan? You saw the whole thing?"

Megan swallowed. "It was pretty dark." She stuffed another cookie into her mouth. *Now you've got me lying, too, Jill. Nice going,* Megan thought.

"Oh, I bet that hurt," Leah said. She got up and stood behind Jill to look at her stitches. "And look at what they did to your hair! That will take forever to grow back! You know, if you combed it all over here and used a barrette..." She moved Jill's hair to one side to cover the stitches.

Jill suddenly jerked her hair out of Leah's hands and stood up.

Leah jumped back. "Oh, I'm sorry, Jill. That must have hurt. I was just trying to help."

Jill glared at her. "It didn't hurt. I'm just tired of everyone telling me what to do. You sound just like my mother. She wanted to

49

cover the stitches up, too. If you don't want to see them, then don't look at them."

Jill stomped out of the cafeteria. Leah's eyes filled with tears. "I didn't mean anything by it," she whispered to Nikki and Megan.

Nikki reached over and squeezed Leah's hand. "We know, Leah."

No, you don't know. But maybe falling down the stairs scared Jill enough to think about what she's doing. Maybe she'll stop drinking now, and no one will have to know what really happened last night. *I wish I didn't know what really happened,* Megan thought.

Keith had heard about Jill's fall, too. He asked Megan questions all through Spanish class. And Megan gave him the same answers.

"I really don't know what happened," Megan told him impatiently. The bell rang to start the class, and Megan pretended to be very busy translating the vocabulary words Mrs. Sanchez had written on the board. One of the words was *fiesta,* which meant party.

Suddenly, Megan remembered that Ryan had invited Jill to a party. But Jill hadn't said if she was going or when the party was going to be. The last time Jill had said anything about Ryan was the first time she had gotten drunk. *There's nothing that I can do to stop Jill, but I hope that she decides not to go with Ryan,* Megan thought.

50

Megan chewed on her pencil. Did Ryan really tell Jill she would feel better if she got drunk? Is that why she decided to drink her mom's rum? And what about the party that Ryan wanted to take her to? Would Jill get drunk again?

"Keith," Megan whispered. "Do you know Ryan Samuels very well?"

Keith shrugged. "Yeah, I guess I do."

"Do you know if he drinks?" Megan asked bluntly.

Keith looked surprised. "Maybe he does. I really don't know."

"Keith, *por favor no hables*," Mrs. Sanchez interrupted.

Megan put her hand over her mouth to hide a grin. Keith never got yelled at by teachers. She thought it did him good to be caught, even if he was one of the smartest kids in the class.

As Megan walked out of the classroom after Spanish class, someone grabbed her arm from behind. "Keith!" she warned him in a stern voice.

"No, it's me," Jill said with a little smile.

"*Que pase?*" Megan asked. She noticed right away that Jill had combed her hair over the stitches, after all. She looked almost normal again. She looked like Jill, her best friend.

"I just wanted to talk to you," Jill said. They

headed toward their lockers. The hallway was already nearly empty. No one ever stayed around long after classes were over for the day.

"I've been thinking," Jill said quietly. "I was a real jerk at lunch today. I know that Leah was only trying to help." She sighed. "I shouldn't have run out of the cafeteria like that."

Jill stopped and turned to face Megan. Her smile was gone. "I've been really rotten to everyone, Megan, especially you. I'm sorry. Really." Her voice dropped almost to a whisper. "Can we still be best friends?" She was trying to smile, but her bottom lip quivered.

Megan hugged her tightly, and Jill hugged her back. Megan could feel tears welling up in her own eyes. "It's okay, Jill," she whispered.

Jill leaned back so they could see each other. A tear was caught in her eyelashes. "It's just that sometimes I feel really down," Jill said softly. "I just keep thinking about what's wrong in my life, like my dad moving out and other stuff."

Jill put her arm through Megan's, and they started toward their lockers. "Sometimes it seems like, I don't know, like my heart is too heavy for my body and it's pulling me down somehow," Jill said. "I don't feel like doing anything anymore—not even swimming."

"You have been a little grouchy lately," Megan admitted. "I've only wanted to be there for you—and to help if I could."

Jill nodded. "I know. Sometimes I think I stay angry on purpose. It seems like when I stop feeling angry, other feelings come back, and I feel even worse." She looked at Megan. "Does that make any sense to you?"

Megan thought of her own father who didn't seem much like a father anymore. "Yes, it makes perfect sense," she answered softly. "I do know what those other feelings are. It's a deep down sad feeling." She took a deep breath. "But my mom says teenagers are supposed to be mixed up and feel bad sometimes, so I guess you're normal. I guess we both are."

When they reached Jill's house, Mrs. Walkerson opened the door.

"I took the afternoon off," she told her daughter with a bright smile. "I thought we could go shopping. We could get a new outfit for the party, okay? We'll find something special that will knock Ryan off his feet." She gave her daughter a quick hug and gently smoothed the hair that covered her stitches. "He's such a good-looking boy!"

"Uh, about that party..." Megan began, but then she changed her mind. *You don't really know anything for sure,* she told herself.

Mrs. Walkerson pretended not to hear Megan and continued with her plan to cheer up Jill. "Oh, Megan, why don't you come with us? I mean, if your mother doesn't mind."

"Oh, I don't think she'd care," Megan said quickly. *Maybe while we're shopping, I'll find the chance to talk to Jill's mom about what kind of party it might be.*

Jill dropped her books on a table in the front hallway and rubbed her forehead with the palms of both hands.

"Well, Jill?" her mother asked cheerfully. "How about it?"

"I'm kind of tired, Mom," Jill said. "I don't think I'm up to it." She turned and walked up the stairs. A minute later they heard her bedroom door close.

Megan and Mrs. Walkerson stood staring up the steps as if they expected Jill to change her mind and come back downstairs.

"I think she has another headache," Megan said with a sinking feeling. "It's a good thing you're taking her to the doctor. Those headaches really are bothering her."

"Megan, I am aware of that." Jill's mother walked stiffly to the front door and opened it. "I am doing my best. That's all any of us can do. When you get a little older, you will realize that."

Megan felt her face burning. She hurried out the front door and ran the two blocks home.

Later that night, Megan lay in her bed wide awake. *If Mrs. Walkerson would just listen to me,* she thought, *she'd change her mind about a lot of things. And she wouldn't be so happy that Jill is going to that party.*

Megan flopped her pillow over to the cool side. She was glad that Jill seemed like her old self today at school. But Jill's mother seemed to push her too hard to be her old self again. She seemed to want her to pretend that everything is just perfect, and that she doesn't miss her father. That can't be helping Jill to get rid of her headaches.

I guess I'm not in charge of Jill's life, either, Megan reminded herself. *I'm just doing my best. And I hope that's good enough.*

Seven

MEGAN sat on the edge of the pool Saturday morning. It seemed like Jill's mood was catching, because she didn't feel much like swimming, either.

She had called Jill the night before to find out what Dr. Simmons had said. "He said that there's nothing wrong," she had said.

"Didn't he take any X-rays?" Megan had asked.

"Why would he do that for just a headache?" Jill had asked.

Megan wondered if Jill told Dr. Simmons how often she got headaches, and how much they bothered her. Jill probably didn't tell him about hitting her head during swim practice, and what caused her to need stitches.

"It was an accident. It was dark." Megan could imagine Mrs. Walkerson explaining everything like it was a fantasy.

I wonder if Jill's father would do anything if he knew about these headaches, Megan thought. Megan had only met Mr. Walkerson three or four times. He traveled a lot for his job.

"Megan, are you going to poop out on us, too?" Leah interrupted her thoughts. Leah was letting water drip off her hands onto Megan's head.

Nikki was standing behind her. "I think it's time for a team meeting," she said.

Megan slowly stood up. She knew Nikki wanted to talk about Jill. She felt bad, because Jill had seemed so cheerful the last couple of days.

"Meg, Coach White wants some restructuring to be done. I agree with him, or our chances at even placing at the district meet are zero," Nikki said.

"Yeah, Coach suggested that we put Gina on our team and see how she does," Leah began. She was talking fast, the way she did when she was nervous. "Do you know Gina? She's so nice and a great swimmer. She swam with us a couple of times last spring before you moved here. She might not be as good as Jill, but..."

"Yeah, with Gina, we might still win," Nikki interrupted. "What do you think?"

"I think that Jill is starting to feel better

now," Megan defended her best friend. "She told me yesterday that she knows she's been hard to get along with. She told me..." The words seemed to stick in Megan's throat. "She told me she really needs friends now. If Gina takes her place, Jill might think that nobody cares about her at all."

Megan looked at Nikki and then at Leah. "We can't just turn our backs on Jill. She really needs us!"

No one said anything for a minute. Finally, Nikki spoke. "I feel bad about this, too, Megan. Jill and I have been friends for longer than you two have, but what can we do? It's what Coach White has decided. It's not our choice." She shrugged her shoulders. "And see, Jill's not here again today. What kind of a teammate is that?"

"Nikki's right, Megan," Leah added. "When she was here the other day, we came in last in the practice relay. And you know that never happens to us. It was so embarrassing."

"There are only three weeks left to practice. Coach had to do something or else pull our team out completely. I'd rather give it our best try with Gina, and then see if Jill can be put back on our team next year," Nikki said.

Megan shifted from one foot to the other. "Let me talk to Jill one more time. If she knew that Coach White wanted to replace her with

Gina, maybe it would shock her into being her old self."

Nikki sighed. "I don't even know if Coach would listen to us if Jill did want to swim in the meet. We're running out of time."

"Remember that Jill is our friend," Leah said softly. "And that does mean a lot."

Nikki glanced across the pool at the coach for a minute. "If Jill comes to the next practice and tries again, then I'll go to the coach with you guys and plead her case."

"Thanks!" Megan said with a big grin. She gave Nikki and Leah quick hugs.

"Next, please." Keith was standing beside the pool in his basketball uniform.

"Next what?" Megan asked.

"Aren't you hugging everybody?" Keith asked with a grin. He stretched out his arms. Leah giggled as she and Nikki walked away.

Megan just looked at Keith. "You must be kidding."

"Well, I guess I can understand why you wouldn't want to," Keith said, pointing to his sweaty basketball jersey.

"How gross," Megan said.

"Hey, just because I don't spend all my time in the water doesn't mean that I'm gross. How's it going, anyway? Have you knocked another second off your relay time yet?"

Megan looked at her feet. "No, we didn't,"

she said quietly.

For once Keith didn't make another joke. Out of the corner of her eye she could see him looking around the pool area. "Where's Jill?" he asked.

"I don't know."

"She ought to be here. You don't have much time left before the meet, do you?" he asked.

Megan shook her head.

"Jill's not doing so hot in algebra, either," Keith told her. "It isn't any fun to beat her on the tests when she doesn't even try." His voice dropped almost to a whisper. "She got the lowest grade in the class on the last test. I saw her paper."

Megan closed her eyes. How could Jill get the lowest grade in the class?

Keith leaned closer to Megan. "She's in trouble, isn't she? When you asked me if Ryan drinks, you weren't just taking a survey. It had something to do with Jill, right?"

Megan finally looked up at Keith. She was surprised to see the serious look in his deep green eyes. She was tempted to tell him about Jill's drinking and about how worried she was. Keith seemed like the only other person in the world who was worried about Jill.

The coach blew his whistle that signaled the end of practice for the day.

"Well?" Keith asked. "Please talk to me."

He grinned down at her.

Behind him Megan could see the rest of the swim team heading for the showers. "It's okay, really," she told him finally. "I have to go." She started toward the showers.

"I'm really good at listening!" Keith called after her.

Megan nodded and kept going. *Well, at least someone else thinks something's wrong with Jill,* she thought.

By the time Megan got dressed, Nikki and Leah had already left. She went outside, shivering as the cold air hit her damp hair. *It's a good thing that the sun's out,* she thought.

Megan saw someone sitting on a bench enjoying the sunshine. But when Megan got closer to the person, her heart sank. It was Jill.

"What are you doing here?" Megan asked her. "Why did you miss practice again?" It was hard to keep the anger out of her voice.

Jill jumped at the sound of Megan's voice. "I didn't hear you coming."

"Practice is over." Megan pointed toward the pool. "You're too late."

"Actually, I got here on time." Jill watched a bird fly by as she talked. "I just decided to stay out here."

Megan's mouth dropped open. "You've

been sitting out here all morning?"

Jill nodded. "I told Mom I was too tired to swim, but she made me come, anyway." Anger flashed in Jill's eyes. "She thinks I was at practice all morning, but she doesn't know everything after all, does she?"

"Jill, staying out here was not a bright thing to do." Megan was getting angry, too.

"Here's something else to think about, Jill," Megan began angrily. "Coach White wants to replace you on our team, because the meet is almost here. I keep defending you to Nikki and Leah, and asking for just a little more time. I keep thinking you'll change your mind and want to win the meet like you used to. But after finding that you deliberately missed practice today, I'm beginning to agree with all of them."

"I don't care if you do ask someone else to swim in the meet," Jill said without emotion.

I am so angry that I should just walk away, Megan told herself. *I should go home and forget that I have a best friend. I need to think about myself for a change.*

"We aren't going to win, anyway," Jill added. "So, it doesn't matter what you decide to do."

"Jill!" Megan knew she was talking too loud, but she couldn't help it. "Aren't you the one who kept telling us to work harder? What happened to all your winning spirit?"

"I was wrong. It just isn't worth it."

Megan grabbed Jill's shoulder. "Stop it! Your parents' divorce isn't the end of the world. Other people manage to live through it and even live to put up with you."

She took a deep breath and loosened her hold on Jill's shoulder. Jill was staring angrily up at her. Her eyes had dark circles under them.

"Look, Jill." Megan tried to stay calm. "You have to pull yourself together. You know we have a good chance to win the district meet, but we can't do it without you. You're the best swimmer on our team. Your mom was right to make you come to practice."

"Oh, sure," Jill said. "She's always thinking about me. Well, I know why she really wants us to win. She hopes she'll get her picture in the paper again. The headline will read 'Karen Walkerson: Mother of the Year.'"

"That's not true!" Megan insisted. "Your mom really cares about you. She was scared to death when you fell down the stairs. And I think she knows you were drinking. I bet she's worried sick about you."

"Ha! She's the one who keeps telling me everything's fine, that everything's normal." She jerked her shoulder out from under Megan's hand. "Anyway, I'm tired of everyone telling me what to do and how to feel—especially my mother. I can't be perfect all the time. Sometimes people just have to be themselves."

Then she faced Megan. "This is me—the real me, not who everybody else wants me to be."

No, it isn't you, Megan wanted to scream at her. *You look awful. Your hair is dirty, and you had the same shirt on yesterday, with the same greasy spots on it. This isn't you at all, Jill Walkerson!*

Megan brushed away the tears that filled her eyes and pulled Jill to her feet. "Come on. Practice is over now, anyway," she said. "I'll walk you home." Jill jerked away from Megan, but she started walking slowly.

Megan looked over at Jill. *This is the same way we've walked home since my family moved here. We used to have so much fun laughing and joking together. But now I can't even remember why I thought we were best friends.*

Jill's mom was coming down the stairs when they pushed open the front door. "How was swim practice? What's wrong?"

Jill glared at her mother. "Nothing's wrong. Everything is just perfect!"

Her mother stopped, halfway down the stairs. Her mouth opened, but no words came out.

I give up, Megan thought. *I have done as much as I can. But I can't do it all. Jill has to give some, too. I'm going home and hide under the covers and pretend this is just a bad dream.*

But as she turned to go, Mrs. Walkerson called her. "Please wait a second, Megan. Is this yours?" She held up a gold bracelet. "It was on Jill's dresser when I was cleaning up."

Jill snatched the bracelet from her mother's hand and pushed past her up the stairs. "Dad gave me this bracelet, so it's none of your business!" she screamed. She ran upstairs, and a second later they heard her bedroom door slam.

Megan could feel Mrs. Walkerson's pain even without looking at her. "Megan?" Jill's mom asked hesitantly. "Was that your bracelet?"

Megan shook her head. "I never saw it before."

"Neither have I, and Jill hasn't seen her father since he..." She closed her eyes. Then she turned and looked at Megan. "I guess you know, anyway," she whispered.

Megan nodded. "I think Jill really misses her dad. I know I miss my dad, too," she added quickly. "He lives in California."

Mrs. Walkerson sat down in the closest chair. "But *I'm* here," she said. Megan could see Mrs. Walkerson's hands shaking. "And I'm taking care of everything. Jill doesn't have a thing to worry about. She doesn't even know what worries are."

Megan said good-bye and quietly let herself out the front door.

She kicked her way through a pile of leaves that had blown onto the sidewalk. *I wish we still lived in California,* she thought. *It didn't hurt so much to be someone's best friend there.*

Her tears made warm streaks down her cheeks, but they quickly turned icy cold.

Eight

JILL wasn't waiting at the corner for Megan on Monday morning. And she didn't show up at their table at lunchtime, either. Megan tried not to think of what else Jill might be doing.

"So, is Jill coming to swim practice today?" Nikki finally asked.

"I'm not sure," Megan answered honestly. "I hope so." She hadn't told them Jill was sitting out on the bench all Saturday morning. Even though she was really angry at Jill for not acting like a friend anymore, she still wasn't ready to give up on her.

Megan really didn't expect Jill to show up at swim practice, but just as the teams were lining up to begin a practice relay, Jill walked into the pool area.

"Gina?" Jill called out. "Aren't you in the wrong place?"

Gina's dark eyes darted from Jill to Nikki.

67

"No, the coach said..."

No one spoke for a second. Then Nikki said, "I'm sorry, Jill. Coach White put Gina on to swim anchor for our team."

"You know we really wanted you, Jill," Megan said quickly. Then she realized Gina was standing right there. "I mean..."

Gina pressed her lips into a thin line. Jill raised her chin an inch or two. She glanced at Nikki and Leah, and then her eyes settled on Megan.

"Jill, if you would have shown up for practices, there wouldn't have been any problem," Megan said.

Jill held up her hand. "Well, I'm done with commitments and promises. No one keeps them, anyway."

What is she talking about? Is she talking about her father?

"Well, I guess that's it," Jill said. "Gina's on the team. I'm off. It doesn't matter, anyway." She started toward the locker room.

"Guys," Megan whispered to Nikki and Leah. "She's leaving for good. We've got to do something."

Nikki shook her head as she watched Jill go. "I don't know what we can do. She just doesn't care anymore."

Leah shrugged her shoulders. "I don't know what to do either, Megan."

"Well, I can't let her go off by herself," Megan told them. "Jill, wait! I'll come with you."

"Megan, we need you over here," Nikki said. She sounded desperate.

Megan pretended that she didn't hear Nikki and hurried after Jill. *If I'm not careful, they'll replace me, too,* she thought.

Jill didn't say a word as she and Megan changed out of their suits. Finally, Megan couldn't stand it anymore.

"Don't you want to be on the team?" Megan blurted out.

Jill tossed her swim suit into the bottom of her locker. "I'm too tired to care."

"I'm not talking about just today," Megan said.

"Let's stop at the Corner Shop on the way home," Jill interrupted. "I need a candy bar or something."

"A candy bar?" Megan repeated. Jill never ate candy bars. But the old Jill never used to miss swim practice or get drunk.

While Jill was busy picking out which candy bar she wanted, Megan looked at the magazine display.

"I saw that!" someone shouted.

Megan looked up as the store clerk grabbed Jill by the arm and shoved her toward the front of the store.

"What are you doing?" Megan asked.

The clerk looked back at her. "You come up here, too. And don't try to put anything back! I'm watching you!"

Put anything back? Megan thought. She looked at her empty hands. *What would I put back? And why is he pushing Jill around?*

Megan hurried to the front of the store. Jill was standing by the counter with her head down and her arms crossed. Her long hair almost covered her face. The clerk kept a tight grip on her elbow as he reached for the phone. He was a skinny kid in a white wraparound apron that almost covered his whole body.

"This is the Corner Shop," he said into the phone. "Yeah, I caught another one. I'll hold her here."

"Hold her?" Megan asked. "What for?"

The clerk ignored her. "I still have to check her friend's purse," he said into the phone.

Megan clutched her purse tightly against her chest. Then she saw Jill's purse laying open on the countertop. In it was a brand new cassette tape still sealed in cellophane. It was Jill's favorite rock group.

"Jill," she whispered. "Tell him that you didn't take that. It must have fallen in your purse."

Jill raised her head and looked at Megan for a brief second. Her eyes were cold. She

70

didn't say a word.

"Jill, tell him!" Megan begged.

"He'll figure it out," Jill mumbled.

"Figure what out?" Megan asked, but Jill looked away.

The clerk finally hung up the phone. He smirked at Megan. "The police are coming."

I've got to do something! What can I do? Megan thought in a panic.

"You're making a mistake," Megan said to the clerk. It was hard to keep her voice from shaking. "Jill wasn't trying to steal that tape. She's got plenty of money for a tape if she wants one."

Megan grabbed Jill's wallet out of her purse and opened it. "Look," she said. "Here's at least $20. She doesn't need to steal anything."

Just then, Megan saw the shiny gold bracelet. It had been hidden beneath Jill's wallet. Jill had said that her father had given it to her as a present. But had he? Megan wondered now. Beside the bracelet sat two sets of earrings still on the cards from the store.

Oh, no, Megan thought. She swallowed hard. *That's why Jill isn't saying anything. She was going to steal the tape—just like the bracelet and the earrings.*

Megan leaned against the counter to steady herself. *Jill, how could you do this? And why?*

The clerk grabbed Megan's purse and opened it. She wanted to rip it out of his hands, but she decided not to. *Maybe he does have a good reason to think I was shoplifting, too.*

Megan watched the clerk paw through her purse. She felt like shaking Jill. *Why are you doing this to me?* she wanted to scream. *Don't you care about me at all? I've been trying to help you!* Megan turned away so the clerk wouldn't see the tears in her eyes.

Suddenly, a flashing red light filled the store. A police car was pulling into the parking lot. As she watched the police car stop in front of the store, she saw two girls standing near the door, watching them. With a sinking feeling, she realized they were in her math class. It was Kate and Shawna. Megan closed her eyes. The news would be all over school by second period tomorrow.

When she looked up again, a police officer was headed straight for them. He was frowning. His stomach hung over his belt, and he had a pair of handcuffs in his hand. Megan's legs turned to rubber.

"I'm sure about this one," the clerk pointed his chin at Jill. "Her friend was probably up to no good, too, but I didn't find anything on her."

"Let me call my mom," Megan pleaded. Her

72

throat was so dry that her voice sounded hoarse. "I didn't do anything."

The police officer pulled the tape out of Jill's purse. "Is this it?"

"Yep," the clerk answered. "We just got those in this morning. And I hadn't sold any of them yet." He sneered at Jill. "She lifted it, all right." He turned to Megan. "What'd you take?"

Megan glared at the obnoxious store clerk.

The police officer turned to the people who were standing around watching. "Listen," he said, "you all just go about your business. We'll handle this."

Megan didn't look up, but she heard shuffling sounds like people moving away.

"Could I please call my mom?" Megan begged.

The police officer, after taking a careful look at Jill, fastened his handcuffs back on his belt. Then he dumped Megan's purse onto the counter. Her lipstick rolled off and onto the floor. *I can't believe this is happening to me. This isn't fair!* she wanted to scream.

"There's nothing in here that I can see," the police officer mumbled. "I guess you can make your phone call."

"Talk louder, Megan," her mother said to her over the phone. "I must not have heard you right." Then she said she'd be right down.

Jill had just glared at the police officer when he told her that she could call home, too. So, Megan called for her.

"Megan, please let me talk to Jill," Mrs. Walkerson said. "I'm sure she can explain what happened."

"I'd like her to explain what happened, too, Mrs. Walkerson," Megan said angrily. "But she won't!"

"I'll be right there," she said finally.

She glanced around the store. Kate and Shawna were gone. *They're probably at home on the phone already spreading the good news,* Megan thought sarcastically.

The police officer let Megan and her mom leave after about an hour of standing around in the store.

"Well," Mrs. Schuster said as she pulled out of the store parking lot, "that was really too bad. I just wish that police officer would have believed us about poor Jill. Sooner or later, he'll have to admit he's wrong and apologize to her."

Both mothers had tried to convince the clerk and the police officer that it was all a misunderstanding. But Jill had kept a stony silence. Jill's mother seemed to think Jill was merely angry at being wrongly accused of shoplifting. "Don't worry, Jill," she kept saying. "We'll get this straightened out."

"It's too bad this had to happen to Jill right now," Mrs. Schuster was saying, "just when she has to cope with her parents breaking up. She really needs to know you're still her friend, Megan."

Megan pretended to look out her side window, but her tears made it hard to see anything.

"Mom, it's really hard to be Jill's friend right now. I've been trying and trying." Megan's throat was so tight that she couldn't talk anymore. Tears slid down both cheeks. Her mother reached over and held her hand as she drove home.

"This must have been terrible for you, Megan, in front of all those people. Thank God that police officer could at least see that you weren't shoplifting." She shook her head. "I still think he's wrong about Jill. Maybe she just put the tape in her purse while she was looking at something else. If she hadn't been so upset, she could have told him what really happened."

Megan wiped her eyes with a tissue that her mother had handed her. "Jill has a new bracelet, too, and new earrings."

Mrs. Schuster stared at the traffic ahead of her for a second. "What are you saying, Megan?"

"I think she was going to steal that tape."

Megan's voice sounded dead.

"Megan! Why would Jill do that?" her mother asked. "Her family has plenty of money. She's so bright, and she has always been so responsible. Why would she suddenly start shoplifting?"

Megan didn't answer. There wasn't any answer.

Mrs. Schuster sighed and shook her head. "You might be right, but I still can't believe it. I wonder if they're going to make Jill and her mother go down to the police station."

Oh, no! Megan thought. *I hadn't even thought of that! Would they put Jill in jail?*

That night as she fell into bed exhausted, Megan couldn't stop worrying about Jill. Was Jill at home in her own bed or in a juvenile home somewhere? Why had Jill turned into such a different person?

Nine

JILL didn't come to school for the next three days, or at least Megan didn't see her there. *Maybe I just missed seeing her,* Megan thought. *I've been too embarrassed about what happened at the Corner Shop to look anybody in the eye.*

Megan had begged her mother to let her stay home. She really did not feel well. But her mom had insisted she get on with her life and not hide out for something that she didn't do.

Megan didn't think the kids at school would see it that way. She spent the first two periods hiding in a shower stall in the girls' locker room. But after a while, her rear end hurt from sitting on the cement. So, she gave up and went to her third period class.

It was just as bad as she had expected. As soon as she walked in the door, everyone stopped talking. She could feel her face

77

burning. *Kate and Shawna had done a terrific job of spreading the news,* she thought. *I wish Mom were here now to tell these kids I don't have anything to feel embarrassed about!*

All of Megan's instincts told her to run, to get away from all this humiliation. But instead she went to the back of the classroom and took a seat. The teacher began discussing the lesson, and Megan let herself become absorbed in what he was saying.

Lunch hour didn't get any better. "Megan, do you really think Jill was going to steal the tape?" Nikki asked.

"I bet it was all just a mistake," Leah offered. "Jill is the most honest person I know. She wouldn't steal anything."

"But what do you think, Megan?" Nikki asked again. "If the police kept Jill and let you go, they must have had a reason."

"Do you think she did it because I took her place on the team?" Gina asked. She had started eating lunch with them, though Megan wished she hadn't. It was bad enough to talk about Jill with Nikki and Leah. She didn't want to say anything to someone who wasn't really Jill's friend.

"I don't know," Megan said finally. Then she threw the rest of her lunch back into the bag. "I have to go."

Spanish class at the end of the day didn't go well, either.

"Hey," Keith said as soon as she sat down. "I heard what happened."

Megan sighed. There didn't seem to be anyone who hadn't heard. All she wanted to do was hear the final bell ring so she could get away from school, away from all the questioning eyes.

"I just couldn't believe that about Jill." Keith shook his head. "I even asked my dad why somebody as smart as Jill would do something really dumb like that."

"Why would your dad know?" she asked.

"He's a social worker at the Easter Seal Rehabilitation Center downtown," Keith explained. "He kind of knows about kids and why they do things—all except me, of course." He grinned at her.

"So, what did he say about Jill?"

"He said that maybe she was upset about something. Maybe she needed someone to help her sort things out." Keith was quiet for a minute, and then he asked, "But did she really do it? Jill just doesn't seem like the type. I know her parents just split up, but still."

"I really don't know," Megan said. There was that question again. People had asked her the same question over and over all day long.

She opened her Spanish book.

Keith leaned closer to her. "I'm sorry, Megan. I didn't mean to make it worse. I like Jill, too. I hope she pulls out of this."

Megan nodded. She looked down at her book so he wouldn't see the tears in her eyes.

"That must have been pretty gruesome for you," Keith said softly, "with the police and all."

Megan nodded again. Out of the corner of her eye, she saw Keith extend his hand out toward hers, but he pulled it back again.

I wish he hadn't pulled away from me, Megan thought. *I really could use a friend to hold my hand right now, even if he is the biggest klutz in the eighth grade.* A big lump in her throat made it hard to swallow.

The bell rang, and Mrs. Sanchez called, "Hola!"

Just in time, Megan thought. *If Keith was nice to me another minute, I would have cried in front of everyone.*

Megan tried to call Jill three times during those days, but each time her mother said that she was sleeping.

How could she be asleep at 3:30 in the afternoon and at 8:00 at night? Well, at least she's not in jail or in a detention center or anything—unless she is, and her mother won't tell me.

On Friday morning, Megan finally spotted Jill walking to school a block ahead of her. Megan breathed a sigh of relief. Jill was back!

"Jill! Wait for me!" she called after her.

Jill stopped and turned. Megan thought she smiled. She hurried to catch up. What would Jill be like this morning? Megan decided that she really didn't care how she acted. She was just glad to see her.

"Oh, I was so worried about you," Megan said. She threw her arms around Jill and hugged her stiff body. "Is everything okay? Are you all right? Did the police finally believe it was all a mistake?"

"It wasn't a mistake," Jill said flatly. "I was going to swipe the tape. I don't know why." She looked at the sidewalk.

Megan closed her eyes at the words. Her suspicions had come true.

"Did you get arrested?" Megan asked in a whisper.

"Kind of," Jill said. "The policeman took my mom and me downtown to Children's Services. That nearly killed her." Jill made a face. "A man there told us to come to a hearing— to decide what to do with me. We had it on Tuesday."

"What happened? What do you have to do?" Megan asked.

"The judge said I had to get counseling."

Her voice started to rise. "At a mental health center of all places." She stopped and put her hands on her hips. "Tell me the truth, Megan, do you think I'm crazy?"

Megan looked at her for a long minute. Jill had lost so much weight that her jeans were hanging on her hips. The only makeup on her face was black smudges under her eyes. She had pulled her hair into a pony tail, but the rubber band was so loose that her hair was hanging out on both sides.

I don't know if crazy is the right word, but there is something wrong with you, Jill, Megan thought. But Megan couldn't bring herself to say those words. If Keith's dad thought that counseling may be the right thing to do, then perhaps the court is right, too.

Jill didn't wait for an answer. She whirled around and started marching toward school. Megan had to hurry to keep up again.

"At least the judge said that my mother had to come to counseling, too!" Jill said proudly. "Now there's someone who really needs it."

I think you're right about that, Megan thought. "When will you start going?"

Jill shook her head in disgust. "I went yesterday. And do you know what my counselor said? She said that I am depressed. Can you believe it? She thinks that I'm depressed because of my parents' divorce. And she even thinks the depression is causing my head-aches."

Jill grabbed Megan's arm. "Have I ever—even one time—complained about my parents' divorce? Have I ever said I missed my dad?" she demanded.

"Well, no, but don't you miss him?" Megan asked softly. "I know I miss my dad a lot."

"Then maybe you're the one who's depressed," Jill told her. "I'm not the least bit depressed. I bet my mom told a whole bunch of lies about me when she talked to Mary Beth by herself. That's what made her think I was depressed."

"Who's Mary Beth?" Megan repeated.

"She's the counselor," Jill said impatiently. "Well, I had the chance to talk to Mary Beth alone, too. And I let her know who really had the problem. I told her about my mom snooping in my room and always criticizing me."

No, you're wrong, Jill, Megan wanted to tell her. *Your mother never criticizes you. She doesn't even realize you have faults—or problems or worries. She thinks you're perfect.*

"Not only that," Jill was saying, "but Mary Beth is going to call my dad today." She pressed her lips together. "Maybe that will get his attention."

"Maybe it will," Megan agreed.

"Anyway, we have to go back to counseling

next week on Monday and Wednesday. If I don't go, they'll tell the judge." Jill rolled her eyes. "Mom wanted to go just once a week, but the judge said we had to go twice at first."

"What does your mom think about the counseling?" Megan asked. *I can just hear her telling the counselor that everything is just fine at home,* Megan thought.

"What do you think?" Jill snapped. "She hates it. I think she wanted to wear a bag over her head when we went to the mental health center yesterday." Jill sighed. "Maybe if I show up there for a week or two, everyone will get off my back about what happened."

"Jill," Megan said as calmly as she could, "I've been wondering about something. That day in the store, why did you get me in trouble, too? That policeman and that stupid clerk both thought that I was shoplifting, too." Megan got angry just thinking about what had happened.

Jill sighed. Her whole body seemed to shrink. "I'm sorry, Megan. I can't believe I did that. I don't know why. I couldn't even think that day—or any day, I guess."

Megan put her arm around Jill's thin shoulders. "Well, it's over now," she said in a shaky voice. "Just please don't do that again. The kids at school have stared at me all week."

"I'm really sorry, Megan," Jill whispered.

"You should give up on me." She rubbed her forehead with one hand. Then she looked back in the direction of home. "I'm going back."

Megan grabbed her arm before she could leave. "Jill, if I could go to school after what happened, so can you," she told her. "Everyone's going to forget about this someday. Things are going to get better."

Jill stared at the sidewalk. Her hair hung in her face. "No," she said quietly. "They aren't."

Megan practically pulled Jill to school, but after she left Jill at her first class, she didn't see her again all day. *This counseling better help—and fast, before Jill gives up on herself.*

Ten

BY the time school was out on Monday, Megan could tell that Jill was changing. She wasn't like the Jill who had been Megan's best friend all year. But she wasn't the cranky, hopeless girl from the last few weeks, either. For one thing, Jill was even taking books home with her.

"You're carrying books," Megan teased her. "What are those for?"

Jill rolled her eyes. "Mary Beth told me this morning that I had to do one thing each day to make myself feel better." Jill sighed. "But she has some strange ideas about what will make me feel better—like doing homework!"

"Oh, you'll get used to it again," Megan told her with a smile. "I just hope you don't make me do homework, too! Yuck!"

Jill smiled a little and shook her head. "You have to make your own decisions. That's what Mary Beth said."

As they walked home, Megan kept sneaking looks at Jill. She had washed her hair and combed it so the bald place from her stitches didn't show. Her socks even matched her shirt for a change. Whatever Mary Beth was doing, it was working.

The next day after school, Jill really surprised everyone. She came to the pool and worked out.

Megan didn't see her at first. Jill was down at the far end of the pool swimming laps. As soon as Megan spotted her, she hurried over to talk to her.

"Boy, am I glad you're here, Jill!"

Jill was gasping for breath. "This is another one of Mary Beth's dumb ideas," she said. "It's not mine. She says that exercise helps get rid of depression. I wish she'd realize that I'm not depressed."

Megan sat down on the edge of the pool. "What is depression, anyway? I thought it was just a feeling that everyone gets sometimes."

"I guess it is and it isn't," Jill said. "Mary Beth said most people get depressed for a while after something bad happens in their lives—like a divorce."

Megan nodded. "Yeah, she's right about that."

"But it's not the end of the world for everybody," Jill explained. Megan waited for her to go on. "Anyway, Mary Beth says that some people just can't pull out of it by themselves. They just keep feeling sad. But I don't feel sad," she said. "I'm just not interested in the same things anymore." She shook her head. "That's why this 'assignment' is so dumb. Five laps to go, and I can quit."

Jill slipped back into the water. Megan hurried over to Nikki.

"Jill's back!" she told Nikki.

"Wait, Megan," Nikki interrupted. "I'm glad she's here, too. But we have less than two weeks until the district meet. Besides, you know it isn't our decision. Coach White selected Gina to swim on our relay team, and that's the way he'll keep it."

"But if Jill really works hard, maybe he'll let her swim with us. She was the best swimmer on our team!" Megan insisted.

"Let's see if she even shows up here again," Nikki said. "Besides, Gina's counting on swimming with us now."

Suddenly, Megan thought of a way to get Jill back on the team. She casually walked into the locker room and waited there until she heard the coach's whistle. Then she limped back into the pool area, keeping her weight off her left leg.

"Ow!" she said as convincingly as possible.

Nikki and Leah rushed over to her. "What's

wrong?" Nikki asked.

Megan could hear panic in her voice.

"I slipped in the restroom. It's my knee!"

"Oh, no!" Leah said. They both helped her over to a bench.

By then the coach was there, too. Megan tried to wince at the right times while he turned her left leg this way and that.

"I don't see any swelling," he said. "How does it feel, Megan?"

Megan smiled weakly. "I think it will be okay, if I just rest for a while."

The coach shook his head. "I hope so. Your team has had enough problems already."

The other teams were lining up for the relay. Nikki was standing with her hands on her hips and a worried look on her face. Out of the corner of her eye, Megan could see Jill at the far end of the pool leaning against the wall. Everyone had to get out of the water to begin the relay.

"Nikki, you can't do a relay with three girls. Maybe Jill's still here." Megan tried to sound as if she'd just thought of that.

Nikki wasn't stupid, though. She stared at Megan for a minute. "Are you sure your knee is hurt?" she asked suspiciously.

She looked down at her knee to avoid Nikki's stare. "I think it will be okay in a few minutes. I just twisted it. I guess we could all just sit out this relay."

Nikki looked over at Jill. "I'm probably going to regret this," she mumbled to herself.

She hurried over to where Jill was standing. Megan saw Jill shake her head. Then Nikki must have asked again, because they both walked over to the team's starting position.

Jill swam anchor, but the team came in third out of five. Megan closed her eyes. *I guess it's just too late. Jill's out of practice and too depressed to give it her all,* Megan thought.

Megan looked up to see Nikki and Gina whispering together. A few feet away, Jill stared at them. Suddenly, Jill pulled herself out of the pool and headed for the locker room. That was the end of the swim team for Jill. And Jill knew it.

The coach's whistle blew again to end practice. Megan hurried into the locker room and stayed close to Jill, but she couldn't think of a thing to say to make things better.

Finally Jill said, "Megan, would you give me some room to breathe?"

Megan took a step back. "I'm sorry. I just wanted you to know I'm here."

"I see you, okay?" Jill said. Her eyes were cold.

Megan moved a couple of feet away, but

she hurried to finish dressing so she could leave when Jill did. *She needs me, even if she won't admit it. She needs to know someone cares about her even if she didn't win the swim relay*, Megan thought.

As they started toward home, Ryan and two of his friends walked by. Megan hadn't seen him in so long that she'd forgotten how blue his eyes were.

"Are you ready for tonight?" he asked Jill.

"Yeah," Jill said.

"I'll pick you up at 8:00," he said with a mischievous grin. "My buddy's got a car. We're going to double with him and his girl-friend."

Megan grabbed Jill's arm. "Let's go. It's getting late," Megan commanded.

"See you later, Jill," Ryan called as Megan pulled her away.

"Jill," Megan said as soon as they were out of earshot, "what kind of party is this going to be?"

"It's going to be a good one, I hope. I need it."

A chill went down Megan's back. "You aren't going to drink again, are you?"

Jill didn't answer for half a block. "I hope so," she finally said.

"You can't!" Megan practically screamed. "Don't you remember what happened last time? You still have a bald spot from the stitches!"

"Who cares?"

"Jill," Megan said in a shaky voice. "I'm begging you not to do it."

Jill stopped walking and looked Megan in the eye. "My mother wants me to go to this party, you know. She thinks it will help me feel better. I hope she's right."

"You know your mother doesn't mean—"

"Here's my house," Jill interrupted.

Megan watched Jill open her front door and go inside. Jill didn't look back.

Megan stood in the cold trying to decide what to do. Jill was doing so well, until that relay. What a great idea that fake knee injury was. Jill felt worse than ever, bad enough to drink her feelings away.

She began walking in the direction of her own house. *I feel pretty rotten myself these days. Maybe depression is catching. Maybe I need some counseling, too. Or, maybe I can talk with Mom about it. Knowing her, though, she'll tell me my feelings are normal. But there is a limit to normal—even for teenagers.*

Suddenly, Megan remembered what Keith had said during Spanish class. He had offered to listen if she needed him. He would understand. He cares what happens to Jill. *And he cares about me*, Megan suddenly realized. A warm feeling spread through her for the first time in a long time.

Megan practically ran the rest of the way home. The house was empty when she got there. On the table there was a note which read, "I'm out getting some groceries. Be back soon—Mom." Megan grabbed the phone book and looked up Keith's number. A woman answered the phone.

"Uh, is Keith there?" Megan asked into the phone.

"Not right now," the woman said. "He's down at the center with his father. Could I take a message?"

"No, I guess not," Megan answered. "Thank you."

She dragged herself upstairs and curled up on her bed. *I must be as sick as Jill is,* Megan thought. *I feel like crying all the time. Maybe I don't even want a best friend if this is how it has to be. It hurts too much.*

Eleven

MEGAN glanced at the kitchen clock for the 10th time that morning. It said 9:45. *I'll wait until 10:30 to call. Jill will have to be up by then.*

Megan flipped on the TV, scanned the channels, and then shut it off again. *Maybe if I walk over to Jill's house, I could tell if they're awake*, she decided. *I just have to find out what happened last night. Even though I don't feel up to it sometimes, I guess I'm still Jill's best friend.*

"I'm leaving for a little while, Mom," she called into the kitchen as she grabbed her coat and headed out the door. A few minutes later Megan was standing on the sidewalk in front of Jill's house. She could see Mrs. Walkerson walking up the front stairs and decided to knock.

As soon as Jill's mom yanked open the front door, Megan knew that she had made a mistake by coming over.

"Jill's still in bed," Mrs. Walkerson said. She crossed her arms. "She won't even get up. Obviously, this counseling isn't helping at all. I don't know why we bother going there."

"Um, I'll come back later."

"You might as well come in," she said. "Maybe you can talk to Jill and convince her to get out of bed."

Megan took a step into the house and saw a bucket of soapy water sitting at the bottom of the stairs. Then she noticed the smell. Someone had thrown up.

Just then, Jill appeared at the top of the stairs in an old bathrobe and bare feet. She held onto the railing and slowly lowered herself onto the first step.

"I heard what you said, Mom. I don't think counseling is helping, either," she said in a hoarse whisper. "I'm sorry about the bathroom. Hi, Megan."

"Hi," Megan answered as she looked at Jill. Jill's eyes looked bloodshot, and there were dark circles beneath her eyes.

"Whatever it is that you talk about with Mary Beth," Mrs. Walkerson was saying to her daughter, "maybe we could do better without it. At least we didn't have this problem before." She pointed toward the bucket.

Oh, yes, you did, Megan wanted to yell at

her. "Mrs. Walkerson—"

"I just made a decision, Mom," Jill interrupted. "I feel pretty awful today. I've learned my lesson. I won't drink anymore."

"You probably didn't even realize it would make you sick. I just hope Ryan was upset by how sick you got," Jill's mom said.

Megan closed her eyes. This is ridiculous. They are like two actors in a bad play. Do they do this when they're alone together, too?

Jill started walking down the stairs. Her mother met her halfway. Megan could see a grimace of pain on Jill's face as they hugged each other.

Mrs. Walkerson leaned back and smiled. "That's my girl. We'll call the mental health center Monday morning and tell them you're feeling much better and that you don't need to go back."

"But didn't the judge say..." Megan began.

"Oh, I'm sure he'll agree with us. All he has to do is look at Jill's school record to see that she's not a criminal. She doesn't need to be punished any longer," Mrs. Walkerson said.

This crazy reasoning was too much. Megan turned around and left. When she got home, her mother was sitting at the kitchen table reading the newspaper. Megan walked over and slumped into a chair.

"I think I need counseling, Mom," she said.

The tears were gathering again. "Maybe I could go instead of Jill."

Megan spilled out the whole story. She told her mom about the fake scene that just took place between Jill and her mother. By the time Megan was talked out, her mom was hugging her tightly.

"I'm sorry that I didn't realize this was so serious," her mother said. She smoothed Megan's hair back from her face.

"I don't know what to do," Megan whispered. "Now Jill's off the swim team for sure. Her mother's going to let her stop going for counseling. And even if the judge doesn't put her in jail or something, I'm worried about what Jill will do next."

Her mom shook her head. "I wish I knew more about depression," she said. "I thought it was just feeling bad about something."

Megan suddenly thought of Keith's father. "I think I know who to call to find out," Megan said. She quickly found the number and dialed.

Keith answered. "Hello," he said.

"Uh, this is Megan."

"Megan!" he said. "You must need some help on your Spanish, right? We have a big test coming up on Monday."

"I forgot about that test," she admitted. "Right now I need another kind of help. Remember when you said your father knew about kids?

"Sure," he said.

"Well, do you think he knows about depression? That's what Jill's counselor says she has."

"I don't know, but I'll ask him." Keith turned away and yelled, "Hey, Dad!" Then he said to Megan, "He'll be here in minute. He was asleep on the couch."

"Keith!" But he was gone already.

But Mr. Kolasky said he didn't mind having his nap interrupted. He was so easy to talk to that Megan ended up telling him the whole story.

"I can see why you're worried, Megan," he said when she had finished.

He understands, she thought. *He knows about these problems, and he understands*! Her throat became so tight that it was hard for her to talk. Her mother reached over and took her hand.

"Do you know why Jill is acting this way?" Megan asked at last. "Is she really crazy?"

"Not at all," he said gently. "Depression is common in teenagers. Most of them just feel sad for a few days after something disturbing like a fight with a friend happens."

"I've felt depressed before. That's for sure," Megan admitted.

"We all do sometimes," he agreed. "But some people, maybe including your friend, feel bad for weeks or even longer. They dwell on what's wrong with their lives and start to lose interest in school and their friends. They kind of lose their ability to have fun. When something good happens to them, they don't even notice. After a while they convince themselves they can't do anything right and nothing is ever going to get better. They stop trying and get even more depressed."

"But doesn't depressed mean sad?" Megan asked. "Jill doesn't seem sad very often. She's angry at everyone, especially her mother."

"That's the way a lot of teenagers try to cope with depression," Keith's father explained. "An adult might just withdraw and sit alone, but teenagers tend to put up a front. They won't admit they feel sad, and yet they're so uncomfortable with the way they do feel that any other feeling seems better."

"Once Jill said she stays angry on purpose," Megan told him.

"She probably does," he said. "Feeling angry is better than feeling hopeless."

"Is that why she gets drunk, too—to cover up her feelings?"

"Probably. Other kids may cut school or run away from home. Didn't I just read about a girl in your school who was caught shoplifting? Was that your friend?"

Megan didn't answer for a minute. "Yes. Did Jill do that because she's depressed?" she finally whispered.

"It's one way some kids try to cope when they're feeling worthless," Mr. Kolasky told her. "Others start driving recklessly or stealing or using drugs. In fact, sometimes everyone's so busy trying to get them to stop shoplifting or using drugs that they don't even realize the cause of the problem, the depression."

"What about Jill's headaches?" she asked. "I guess the counselor said the depression is causing those, too."

"It might be. Sometimes kids have trouble sleeping or they sleep all the time. They stop eating or they eat too much. They might have stomachaches or backaches or a whole lot of other symptoms. You told me Jill went to a doctor for her headaches, and he didn't find anything. It could be the depression that's causing her headaches."

"Is she ever going to be okay again? Do kids ever get over depression?" Megan asked.

"Sure they do," he told her. "Some kids manage to get better on their own. And sometimes they have someone who helps them feel better about themselves."

"I've been trying to help Jill," Megan said

as her voice cracked.

"I'm sure you have. And you probably have helped Jill more than you know. But her feelings can be very overwhelming and scary to her," he explained.

"But what else can I do for her?" Megan asked.

"All you can do is just what you have been doing—be her friend," he said.

Megan swallowed hard. "She makes it so hard sometimes."

"I'm sure she does, but just remember that Jill's depression is in no way your fault. It isn't anybody's fault. It just happens to some people, including some teenagers."

"But why?" she asked.

"There can be a lot of causes," Mr. Kolasky explained. "From what you've told me, Jill was a top student before this happened. Maybe she always expected too much of herself. Maybe when she felt bad about her parents' divorce, she tried to deny her feelings and pretend they weren't there. That usually doesn't work for very long."

"Her mother won't even admit anything's wrong," Megan added.

"That certainly makes it hard for Jill to admit it then. Maybe she thinks she'll disappoint her mother if she feels sad about the divorce. Maybe deep down she's afraid her mother will leave her, too, just like her dad did."

"Poor Jill," Megan whispered.

"Just be her friend, Megan," Mr. Kolasky repeated. "Encourage her to go back to her counselor. Help her feel better about herself. That's all you can do. Don't expect so much of yourself."

Megan didn't say anything.

"Any time you want to talk about this again, please give me a call," he suggested. "You can call me at the rehabilitation center, too, if you like. They won't mind at all. Okay?"

Megan took a deep breath, "Okay."

"Keith seems to want the phone, Megan, so I'll let him talk with you again."

"Megan," Keith began, "I just wanted to say that you can call me, too. In fact, would you like to go to the movies with me this afternoon—just to take your mind off everything?"

"The movies?" She was so tired it was hard to think.

"If you want to," Keith mumbled. "I just thought..."

"Maybe we could go another time, okay, Keith?" she asked.

"Right," he said quickly. "Bye."

Megan stared at the phone. *Maybe I should have said yes*, she thought. *Maybe he won't ask again. But I hope he does.*

Twelve

THE next morning Megan was waiting for Jill at the usual corner before school. Megan spotted Jill as she rounded the corner and headed her way. *Just be Jill's friend like Keith's father said*, Megan told herself. *That's all you can do.*

"Hi!" Megan called to her.

As Jill came slowly closer, Megan saw that the circles around her eyes were deeper. Her shirt and jeans both seemed too big for her.

When Jill finally reached the corner, she held out a bag to Megan. "Here," she said with a tired smile. "You can have it."

Megan opened the bag and saw Jill's lunch.

"You need to eat this, Jill," Megan said.

Jill shook her head. "No, not today."

They started walking toward school.

"You have really lost a lot of weight," Megan commented. "I wish I could lose some, too." She patted her stomach.

"No, you don't," Jill practically whispered. "It's not worth it to feel this way."

Should I say it? Megan asked herself. *Here goes...*

"Uh, you might feel better if you kept going to counseling," she suggested. "Mary Beth seems like a nice person."

"No, I'm not going to go to any more counseling. It upsets Mom too much."

"Jill—"

Jill waved her hand at Megan. "Talking doesn't help."

At lunchtime, Megan had the feeling that she didn't belong at their usual table anymore. Standing in the doorway to the cafeteria, she could see Gina talking a mile a minute to Nikki and Leah.

Megan looked all around, but she couldn't spot Jill. She had Jill's lunch bag in her hand to give back to her. Megan walked over to the closest door and looked out at the bench where Jill had sat that Saturday morning when she skipped swim practice. There was something or someone on the bench.

Megan hurried to her locker and grabbed her coat. She saw that Jill's coat was still in her locker, so she took it with her just in case.

As she walked closer, she saw that the figure was Jill. She was sound asleep on the bench. Megan carefully covered her with her coat. Then she sat at the end of the bench and started eating her own lunch.

Seeing Jill asleep reminded Megan of all the times they had stayed overnight together—like the time they made brownies at Megan's house at 3:30 in the morning. They'd both fallen asleep, and the brownies had started to burn, setting off the fire alarm. She remembered her mom nearly flying down the stairs. As soon as everyone had gotten over being scared that the house was on fire, Jill and Megan started laughing like crazy. Then they ate the brownies.

Megan sighed. Life was sure simpler then and a lot more fun.

The bell rang. Lunch period was over.

"Jill," Megan said softly. "It's time to go to class."

Jill opened her eyes wide and looked around in a panic, but then she realized where she was. She closed her eyes again.

"I'll just stay here," she said. "I don't learn anything in class, anyway."

Megan pulled her to her feet. "You still have to go. If I have to sit in class, then so do you." She forced a smile. "You'll be sorry for all those times you made me go to class!"

"I am sorry," Jill mumbled. "It was a waste of time."

Megan took Jill's arm and guided her back

into the building.

Megan didn't have a chance to talk to Keith in Spanish class because the test began right when they walked into class. Megan realized that she'd forgotten all about the test.

At practice after school, everyone talked about the big district meet on Saturday. The screaming during the practice relays was deafening. Their team finished first. There was hope for the district meet, after all.

Nikki and Leah and Gina hugged each other and jumped around. Megan tried to join in, but her heart wasn't in it. They had already forgotten about Jill.

The big surprise of the day came right after dinner. Megan answered the phone, and Mrs. Walkerson was on the other end.

"Jill and I are going over to the mall," she said. "Do you want to come with us? You and Jill could look around while I do some shopping of my own."

Megan was so surprised by the call that she didn't answer right away. "Sure," she said finally. "I think that would be fun." Megan knew it wouldn't be fun at all, but she wanted to keep an eye on Jill.

When they got to the mall, Jill's mom asked them to meet in an hour near the fountain.

"Where do you want to shop?" Megan asked. She was having trouble acting cheerful.

Jill just shrugged her shoulders.

"Let's start at our favorite store," Megan suggested. "I've got some money. If I can find a cute outfit on sale, you can wear it, too."

Megan scanned a rack of sweaters that were on sale. She pulled out a soft peach one. "How about this one, Jill? Do you like it?"

But Jill had wandered away. She stood near the store's front window watching the people walk by. "Jill," Megan called to her. "Do you think Keith would like this color?" Megan smiled a real smile for a change.

Jill just stared at the sweater Megan was holding.

"I want to look in the department stores," she said.

"Okay." Megan was glad that Jill was interested in something. That was a good sign. She put the sweater back and hurried after Jill.

As they entered the department store, Megan noticed a sign that announced a shoe sale. "Hey, I wonder if they have some neat sneakers on sale," she said to Jill.

Jill waved her hand to show that she had heard and walked further into the store. Megan didn't find any shoes she liked. She finally gave up and looked around for Jill. She was nowhere in sight. Megan walked through the cosmetic department, around the handbag department, and the scarf department. Twice she saw kids she recognized from school, but Jill seemed to have disappeared.

Megan started to move through the store more quickly. Where could she have gone?

When Megan walked around the end of a jewelry counter, her breath caught in her throat. Jill was standing there filling her purse with bracelets off a stand.

Megan rushed over. "Stop it!" she whispered hoarsely. Just then an older woman in a raincoat walked over to the same counter and started looking at earrings.

Jill put another bracelet into her purse.

Megan grabbed Jill's arm and squeezed it. "Put those back, Jill," she whispered through clenched teeth. "And hurry up!"

The woman beside them turned her head a little and watched what they were doing.

Oh, no, Megan thought, *not again.*

Megan let go of Jill's arm and took a step backward. *I should leave right now and let Jill get caught by herself this time*, she thought. *I could find a phone and call my mom to come and get me. She'd understand why I had to leave.* If Mrs. Walkerson had to face the police by herself, she might finally realize that Jill needs help.

But maybe the judge wouldn't send Jill for counseling the second time around. Maybe he'd put her in a detention center for juvenile deliquents. Or, maybe he'd decide that her mother can't control her and put her in a foster home or someplace like that. How would Jill feel then? What would she do?

Will you, Megan Schuster, be sorry for the rest of your life that you didn't help your best friend when she needed you most?

The woman in the raincoat was staring now. Her eyes were narrow slits of suspicion.

Jill picked another bracelet off the rack on the counter.

"Jill!" Megan grabbed her hand again. Jill glared at her without letting go of the bracelet.

Just be her friend, Mr. Kolasky had said.

How can I be her friend when she keeps doing this to me? Who is going to believe that I'm not shoplifting if I get caught twice in two weeks? Maybe the police will put handcuffs on both of us this time. Maybe we'll both end up locked in a detention center.

The woman suddenly stepped back from the counter and started looking frantically around. *She thinks that we're shoplifting for sure now. She's trying to find a sales clerk or the store security people.*

Megan felt her heart beating a hundred miles a minute. *I've got to help Jill—and fast.*

Thirteen

MEGAN stood paralyzed for a minute. Then she grabbed Jill's purse and turned her back so the woman in the raincoat couldn't see what she was doing. She took the bracelets out of Jill's purse and shoved them back on the rack.

"Wait!" Jill said angrily. "I want those! I need them!" She reached for the bracelets. "Leave me alone!"

Megan caught her hand and held it tight. "If I weren't your best friend," she whispered hoarsely, "I might."

Megan pushed Jill around the jewelry counter, away from the woman and toward the mall entrance. *Everyone in the store must be watching us. We probably won't even make it to the door*, she thought. She tried to blink away the tears that were making it so hard to see.

"Hey!" the woman in the raincoat yelled.

"They're getting away."

Megan nearly bolted for the door. Don't run. Don't look back. Try to pretend that she isn't talking about us.

Megan hurried Jill out the door and into the mall. A little way down the corridor, Megan ducked into another store pulling Jill along with her. Megan moved behind a table piled high with sweaters and pretended to look at them while she watched the people walking back and forth outside the store. Her heart was still beating wildly.

"Let me go!" Jill tried to wrench her arm away from Megan. "You don't know what you're doing!"

Megan kept a tight grip on her. "I do know that I'm taking an awful chance because I'm your friend, Jill," she whispered. "Just stand here a minute until we see if you—*if we*—get caught this time."

Megan tried to look interested in the sweaters and watch everyone who came into the store. After a minute or two a tall, thin man in a hooded sweatshirt walked in and looked right at them. Was he a policeman in disguise? Megan swallowed hard and put her head down.

"Do you like this one?" she asked Jill, trying to keep her voice from shaking. Jill just stood there and glared at her.

The man walked back out of the store. She glanced at her watch. It was five more minutes until Mrs. Walkerson was supposed to meet them. *Maybe we can get out of here without being arrested. I can see the fountain from here, but if that woman in the raincoat sees us, she may start yelling again.*

She turned to tell Jill they would stay put in the store for a few more minutes. But Jill was staring at the floor. All the anger seemed to have vanished from her face. She looked like she had given up trying to deal with everything. Jill's arm was so limp that Megan felt like she was holding her up instead of keeping her from getting away.

Just then Mrs. Walkerson walked by the store entrance and headed for the fountain.

"Mrs. Walkerson!" Megan called, trying to keep her voice calm.

"Oh, here you are!" Jill's mom said as she came into the store. "Did you buy anything? Jill, what's wrong?"

Jill glanced up at her mother and then went back to staring at the floor.

"Could we just go home?" Megan asked quickly.

"Wait a minute, Megan. Jill?" her mother asked again. "Don't you feel well?"

"That's it," Megan agreed. "She's sick. Let's take her home."

During the short ride home, Jill sat between them on the front seat. She stared at the lights of the traffic without blinking. She wouldn't talk. Her mother was getting frantic.

"Jill! Tell me what's wrong!" her mother pleaded.

"Everything's perfect, Mom," Jill finally mumbled. "It's just the way you wanted it."

Mrs. Walkerson didn't say anything for a minute. Finally, she turned to Megan.

"Megan, do you know what's wrong?" Mrs. Walkerson asked in a shaky voice.

Megan took a deep breath. "Yes. Jill tried to steal some bracelets from the department store. When you saw us, we were hiding from the police."

Mrs. Walkerson's mouth dropped open. A horn blasted at them as the light turned green.

Jill's mom shook her head. "Jill, I would buy you a bracelet if you really wanted it. You know that!"

"I don't think that's the problem, Mrs. Walkerson," Megan continued softly. "I think Jill was going to take every bracelet on the counter. She already had four of them in her purse."

Megan felt really strange talking about Jill as if she wasn't even sitting inches away.

"Jill, why would you do that?" her mother

asked. "After what we just went through last week? If your father finds out, he might think I can't..." Her voice broke. "And the judge warned you what would happen if you got in trouble again. Oh, this can't be happening!" Mrs. Walkerson jerked the car to a stop in their driveway.

Jill glanced at her mom and opened her mouth, but closed it again.

"I think Jill needs to go back to counseling," Megan said softly. "I have talked with someone about depression and how serious it can be. I really think that Jill needs some help to get through this."

Mrs. Walkerson looked up at Megan for a minute. Then she put her arm gently around her only child and pulled her close.

"I guess you do need help," Jill's mother whispered. She kissed Jill's cheek. "I tried, but..."

"I tried, too," Jill finally said. She spoke so softly that it was hard to hear her. "But I just couldn't do it. It's too hard."

"What's too hard, Jill? What do you mean?" her mother asked.

"I just can't be perfect," Jill said.

Megan glanced down at her watch. "Mrs. Walkerson, it's only 7:45. Do you think the mental health center is open tonight? We could call and see if Mary Beth is there.

Maybe she could help tonight."

Mrs. Walkerson stared at Jill for a minute. Then she nodded. "I guess we'd better. I called them this morning and said Jill didn't feel well and couldn't come for her appointment," she said in a tired voice. "I guess I didn't realize how bad she felt."

They went into the house and immediately dialed the center. Mary Beth was there and told them to come right over.

After Jill's mom hung up the phone, she turned to Megan. Her eyes were red-rimmed, but her voice wasn't shaking anymore. "Would you come with us, Megan?" she asked. "Somehow I think you know more than I do about what's going on. And you are Jill's best friend, that's for sure."

Megan didn't trust her voice to talk, so she just nodded. She called her mom to tell her what was happening.

As soon as the three of them walked into the waiting room at the mental health center, a young woman wearing a long skirt and boots hurried over to them. She reminded Megan of an older Jill.

Mary Beth hugged Jill tightly. To Megan's surprise, Jill hugged her back.

"I'm glad you're here," Mary Beth told Jill.

"Me, too," Jill whispered.

Mary Beth smiled. "Why don't you all come

back to one of our conference rooms?" she asked. "We can talk there."

She led them to a comfortable room that looked a lot like a living room. Megan gratefully collapsed in a soft easy chair, and Jill and her mom sat close together on a couch.

Mary Beth talked for a few minutes about depression and how it makes people feel really down. She reminded them that teenagers in particular do things that they ordinarily wouldn't do just to try to feel better.

"I guess you explained that before," Mrs. Walkerson admitted. "But I thought you were wrong about Jill. I guess I had an excuse for everything that had happened. So, I didn't listen."

"Listening is one area we could work on," Mary Beth said gently. "That and saying what you really feel. You know, going through a divorce is hard on everyone. You both have a right to feel sad about it. But you need to help each other when you feel sad instead of pretending everything's okay. Your feelings are real. And it's okay to express them."

Megan glanced over at Jill and her mother. They were holding each other tightly and trying not to cry.

Mrs. Walkerson took a deep breath. "My family has never been very good at sharing feelings. My parents always made us feel bad if we cried or told them anything bad that had happened to us. My brother has the same problem that I do. He doesn't find it very easy to express anger or sadness."

She sat silently for a minute and then went on, "Sometimes he goes into bouts of sadness. I guess my style is to carry on as if nothing ever happens. I guess I cope best that way."

"A lot of doctors and psychiatrists think depression is at least partly genetic," Mary Beth explained. "It often runs in families. It sounds as if your uncle has it, too, Jill."

Jill stared at her, as if she were still thinking it over.

Mrs. Walkerson sighed. "Jill, I do want to help you to feel better." She hugged her daughter tightly. A tiny smile softened Jill's thin, tired face.

"Jill will recover from this if she gets help," Mary Beth told them. "But both of you really do need to come to counseling."

"I know," Jill's mother agreed. "I see that now."

Mary Beth then looked at Jill. "And you'll have to do my assignments, too, no matter how dumb you think they are."

Jill really did smile then. *How can her smile make me want to cry?* Megan wondered.

"I'm sure that you will still have some ups and downs, though," Mary Beth warned them.

"There will be some angry days and some doubts."

"Well, I'm going to work hard at not pretending," Mrs. Walkerson said. "That should help us both. Life might actually be easier that way, after I get used to it." She turned to her daughter. "If I promise to tell you when I feel bad, will you promise to tell me when you do?"

"Even when I miss Dad?" Jill asked her.

Mrs. Walkerson closed her eyes for a second. Then she nodded. "Even then. You know I miss him, too." She put her hand over her mouth as tears slid down both cheeks.

"Could you both come back in the morning?" Mary Beth asked Jill and her mom. "It's getting kind of late now, but I think we need to talk some more. Then we can go back to our regular appointment times."

As they all stood to leave, Jill hugged her mother. "I really am glad you're there for me," she said softly.

Fourteen

THE next day when Jill walked into the school cafeteria at lunchtime, Megan saw that Jill's hair was in a French braid. "My mother helped me do it," she said with a little smile.

Jill had spent an hour that morning with Mary Beth, and Megan could tell that she felt pretty good about it. Megan wasn't sure that sitting at their regular table for lunch was such a good idea. But Jill insisted.

"I promised that I would tell you all something," Jill said as soon as she sat down. "It's really my assignment for today." Megan noticed that Jill looked a little embarrassed.

"This morning I started going to counseling. Actually, I went a couple of times before, but I wasn't really listening then. Anyway, Mary Beth, my counselor, says I will feel a little better every day if I do my assignments. So, today I'm supposed to tell you why I've been so grouchy lately." Jill bit her lip, and Megan held her breath.

"I have a condition called depression. It's a lot like the times you feel depressed, but it's harder for me to stop being depressed. Sometimes I just think about the things that are wrong in my life and don't notice the good things. And sometimes I pretend things are okay when I really feel terrible. But I'm going to get better."

"My mom suffers from depression, too," Gina admitted quietly. "I don't say much about it, because most people don't understand. They think it means she's crazy or something, and she's not at all. She used to sit around on the couch all day without saying anything. And we couldn't figure out why for a long time."

"Does she go to counseling, too?" Jill asked.

"She did for a while, and it really helped," Gina answered. "After a while she started feeling so much better that she went out and got a job. So, now I'm stuck making dinner." She smiled.

"My mom still takes medicine to help keep her from becoming so depressed again," Gina continued. "Will you have to take medicine, Jill?"

"I don't think so," Jill answered. "Mary Beth says she thinks I can get better without it.

She said that doctors don't like to give it to kids unless it's really necessary. She told me this morning, though, that some doctors think depression has something to do with the chemicals in your body. They get out of balance and make you feel bad. I guess certain kinds of medicine help the chemicals get back in balance."

Jill took a deep breath and looked around the table. "So, I guess that's it. I hope I won't be so crabby now, but I might be. This will take a while."

When Megan got to Spanish class, Keith was waiting to talk to her. "Hey, listen to this!" he said excitedly. "Jill asked me to help her catch up on her algebra. I'm going over to her house after school. I thought she'd given up on algebra. Isn't that great?"

Megan was stunned. "Yeah, that's great," she muttered. But suddenly Megan realized that she really didn't think it was so great. *Could I be jealous that Keith will be helping Jill?* Megan wondered.

Megan opened her Spanish book and pretended to study. *I should be happy that Jill cares about schoolwork again.*

She noticed that Mrs. Sanchez was passing out the Spanish tests they'd taken recently. When Megan finally got enough courage to turn hers over, it was as bad as she expected. She got a *C-*.

At swim practice after school, Megan's team won a practice relay by several seconds.

"Hey!" Nikki said excitedly. "We're really cooking now. We're going to win on Saturday! I just know it!"

"I wonder if Jill will come and watch us, now that she's feeling better," Leah said. "What do you think, Megan?"

Keith and Jill are probably sitting down to study about now. They're sitting at her kitchen table eating cookies. Keith is surely noticing how nice Jill looks with her hair in a French braid.

"Megan!" Leah said louder.

"What?" she asked angrily.

Nikki squinted at her. "Megan, what have you been thinking about all afternoon?" she asked.

Megan shrugged.

"Well, what do you think?" Leah asked again. "Do you think Jill will come to the district meet to watch us?"

"I don't know," Megan answered. "She might have a date or something."

"A date?" the other three girls said together.

Megan blushed. "I mean, maybe we should tell her we want her to come."

The next morning on the way to school,

Megan was determined not to ask Jill about Keith. But she couldn't help it.

"How's your homework coming?" she asked her, trying to sound as if she were just wondering.

"It's funny you should ask," Jill answered. "But it's not too funny." Megan noticed she wasn't laughing. "I have a report due today in language, and I didn't get it done. Maybe I'll never catch up."

"Does Mary Beth know about your report?" Megan asked. "Maybe she can help."

Jill smiled a little. "Does she know anything about Edgar Allan Poe's poems?"

Megan rolled her eyes. "I mean, maybe she could talk to your teacher. Your teacher must have noticed you were...having trouble. I bet she'd be glad to give you some extra time."

Jill frowned. "I hate to hand anything in late."

Megan shook her head. "Give yourself a break, Jill. Believe me, the world doesn't stop if you turn something in late. I tried it more than once, and I know."

"I guess you're right," Jill said. "Maybe I'll ask my language teacher myself—just this once."

"So, how's your algebra coming?" Megan asked. As soon as she said it, Megan felt like biting her tongue. *You had your chance with*

Keith, and you blew it. Now it's Jill's turn with him, she told herself.

"Oh, algebra's going pretty well. I'm almost caught up."

Megan decided to change the subject. "We all hope you'll come to the meet on Saturday," she said. "You really are still part of our team, you know."

"It's this Saturday? Oh, Keith asked me...I can't believe I forgot about the meet."

I just knew it, Megan thought. *And the other girls thought I was being funny when I told them Jill couldn't come to the meet because she had a date. The joke's on me.*

Megan managed to be polite to Jill at lunchtime. She pretended she was happy that Jill's language teacher gave her two more days to do her report.

By Spanish class, Megan had almost convinced herself that Keith was still the big klutz she always thought he was.

"Megan, hi," he said. "Hey, you should see how well Jill is doing in algebra now. She got a *B* on her test today."

Megan opened her Spanish book to discourage Keith from telling her more.

He kept talking anyway. "The best part is, Jill is going to come with me on Saturday."

Megan sighed. *I bet he doesn't even remember the day he asked me to go to the movies,* she thought. "That's terrific," she told him, trying to sound sincere.

"Wait until she sees the smiles on those kids' faces. They love it when teenagers pay attention to them," Keith said.

Now Megan was confused. "What kids?"

"The ones at the rehab center," he explained. "Jill is going with me to help them do exercises and play games. They always need more volunteers. It was really my dad's idea to bring Jill along."

"Jill is going to go volunteer with you at the rehabilitation center on Saturday?" she asked.

"Isn't that great?" Then Keith leaned closer to her. "Do you think you would have time to come, too, Megan? I would have asked you before, but you're always so busy with swim team and everything."

"Me?"

He smiled. "I think you'd be great with those kids. Anyone who could stick with Jill through this whole thing could really help the kids at the center, too."

Megan grinned until she thought her face would split. "I really would like to, Keith, but..."

He nodded. "I knew it. You're busy."

"I sure am! It's the big district meet on Saturday. Why don't you come and watch it? Then next weekend we can all go down to the rehabilitation center."

"The meet! I forgot all about it," he said with a grin. Then he suddenly looked very serious. "Are you sure you want me there, Megan?"

Megan smiled. "I'm sure."

They all went together to the swim meet. Jill, her mom, and Keith rode with Megan and Mrs. Schuster for the two-hour trip. Megan thought Jill was a little quiet on the way up, but when their team won—just barely—Jill seemed really glad.

Megan spotted the whole gang sitting over on the bleachers. She hurried over to them with dripping hair and all.

"We won! Just like you said, Jill! We won this year!" Megan yelled. Then she said, "Next year, Jill, you'll be swimming with us."

"A five-person team?" Jill asked. "The judges will throw us out."

Everyone laughed.

"You know what I mean," Megan said. "We'll work it out somehow. You'll be our anchor. We'll set a record next year!"

Suddenly, Jill looked very serious. "I knew you would win, Megan," she said. "So, I brought my own trophy for you." She handed Megan a small box.

Megan noticed that both mothers and Keith had big smiles on their faces.

"Hey!" Megan said. "Does everyone know what's in this box but me?"

"It could be," Keith told her.

"Come on, Megan. Open it," Jill insisted.

Megan carefully pulled the lid off the box. Nestled inside was a small silver trophy with an engraved inscription. When she read it, she had to bite her lip to keep from bursting into tears in front of everyone.

The fancy inscription on the trophy read, "Megan Schuster, My Best Friend."

About the Author

LINDA BARR loves to write! She enjoys writing both fictional books and nonfiction educational books for children and teenagers. Her favorite books to write are those that deal with real problems and issues affecting teenagers and children.

"The problems some people have to face every day are tougher than anything I could make up. I hope my readers will see that almost always there is hope and there is help," says Linda.

Linda lives in Columbus, Ohio, with her husband, Tom, and their own teenagers, Danny and Colleen. *Best Friends Don't Tell Lies* is Linda's fourth book for Willowisp Press. She also wrote the best-selling *I Won't Let Them Hurt You.*